PASS THE URN DAY

SHERI DUFF

ISBN: 978-1-7369138-0-2

Cover Art by Oliviaprodesign

Sheriduffbooks.com

For Dani.

You are the light of my life!
You are my moon and stars.
You are my sun.
You are my blue sky.
You are the sweetest pitter-patter of the rain that helps all the flowers grow.

Forever,
Your Nana

"Birds sing after a storm; why shouldn't people feel as free to delight in whatever sunlight remains to them?"

~Rose Kennedy

PROLOGUE ~ AN URN OR A BOX?

Julia Larsen, known to her family as Bessa, a name given to her by Letti, sat on the brightly colored chaise lounge with her laptop, searching for urns. She tugged at the worn quilt her own mother had made so long ago, pulling it off her feet. "These suck," she said, scrolling through the website.

"What sucks?" Letti, her favorite—and only—six-year-old granddaughter tried to look at the screen.

"Vases," Bessa said.

Letti climbed up the side of the couch and plopped next to her grandmother, taking a piece of the quilt between her fingers and rubbing the soft fabric. The two of them, although fifty-nine years apart in age, looked like they were the same weight. Pancreatic cancer was taking Bessa. Bessa wore pants with drawstrings so she could cinch them, forcing them to stay on her body. She owned an assortment of these pants in various colors, all but black. Sporting tie-dye sweats and a t-shirt that read *Don't be a Richard,* she typed in a new search.

"Why do you need a vase?" Letti asked.

Bessa kissed the top of Letti's head and then inhaled the

strawberry-scented detangling solution used to comb through her pile of chestnut curls. “Because when I die, they need to put my ashes somewhere. Remember how we talked about that?”

“Will you fall out of the vase?” Letti asked.

“Nope. These have lids.”

“It should be pretty like you, Bessa.” Letti touched her grandmother’s cheek.

“I want something fun,” Bessa pat Letti’s hand, then continued to scroll. “None of these are right.”

Alex, Letti’s mom, Bessa’s daughter-in-law, walked from the kitchen to the family room and peeked down at the computer. “What the heck?”

“UrnsForU.com,” Bessa pointed at the screen of all things death: urns, headstones, and cremation keepsakes for family *and* animals.

“Seriously?” Alex exclaimed.

“I will die. Sooner than later. We need to get this done and I don’t want anyone but me planning this funeral. If my kids have a say in it,” Bessa rolled her eyes like a teenager, “nothing will be the way I want. They *will* stress. I don’t want them to have to worry about anything. Funerals are ridiculous, but they’ll do it, anyway. They never listen.”

Alex leaned in closer and said, “They all have an opinion, that’s for sure.”

“I like the purple one,” Letti said.

Alex studied the options. “I like the pink speckled one.”

“No, the purple one.” Letti squirmed before touching the screen again.

Bessa pulled Letti close, “It looks like a bunch of stars swirling in the sky. Did you know the universe goes on and on forever?”

“What’s the universe?” Letti asked with her eyes open wide.

“The stars.” Bessa moved her face closer to Letti.

“Do speckles go forever?” Letti asked.

“Nope.” Bessa smirked.

Letti leaned forward. Her left brow rose. “Don’t get the speckles.”

“Time for bed, Sugar Plum.” Alex said.

“I’m not a sugar plum.” Letti yanked at the quilt and covered her face.

Bessa flipped the white quilt with hand-stitched granny squares off of her and then tickled Letti before slowly getting up from the couch. “Come on, Snuggle Bunny, I’ll read you a story.” Bessa held out her hand, which Letti took without argument.

Alex lifted the quilt off the chaise lounge and folded it before setting it back on the arm of the chair and whispering under her breath, “How are we going to survive without you?”

1. THE FIRST LETTER

Father Joe, the last to leave the reception, handed Alex a purple envelope on his way out of her and Lukas' home. "Bessa wanted me to give this to you. She asked that you read it to the family—once everyone left." He paused, tilted his head and smirked. "She wanted all of you to gather on the Saturday after the service to read it. But she said none of you would wait. And she may have said you were all a pain in her ass."

Alex let out a quick puff of air through her nose and giggled. "I'm sure she did."

Father Joe then handed Alex a smaller, pink envelope. "This is for Letti."

Alex could feel the lump in her throat when she swallowed. It felt like the on start of a cold, but what she probably needed was more water. She held on tight to the envelopes. "Thank you. For everything, Father."

"I'm a phone call away if you need anything," The priest paused, then said, "Or you could come to mass with Lukas and Letti."

"I'll do that," she said, knowing full well she wouldn't.

Mass was not Alex's thing. She went on the holidays, and for the important rituals for Letti, but that was it. Letti went with Lukas and Bessa when Bessa was alive. Alex knew Lukas would continue the tradition for his mother.

Alex placed two fingers on her right temple. She walked back into the house where her daughter, Letti, her husband, Lukas, and his siblings, Jens and Nora sat on the sectional in the living room. The siblings—clones of their parents—all inherited the soft brown hair color their mom once had, and their father's light blue eyes. Bessa had instructed everyone to wear denim and bright colors for her service. They wore denim, but Lukas and Jens both decided on charcoal colored button-down shirts. Only the tags on them were different. Lukas' read Ariat, while his brother Jens sported the Hugo Boss label.

Nobody, not even the dog, sat on the chaise lounge with the quilt draped over it. It was the one of pieces of furniture Bessa had given to Lukas and Alex when they bought the house from her when the cancer invaded her body. Bessa had insisted they make the house theirs. Alex felt guilty at first, but when Bessa brought home paint strips, they had a blast picking out colors. Both Alex and Bessa loved color. Alex painted each room a different color, and Bessa finally got her plum bedroom down in the basement where it was cooler. She liked it that way. She also had the biggest bathroom in the house.

Lukas stared out the window toward Pikes Peak, and Alex wondered if he even noticed the beautiful day and the way the snow perfectly capped the top of the mountain. His sister, Nora, rested her head on his shoulder. Letti, whose pigtails were falling out, found comfort curled up in her Uncle Jens' arms. One of her hands held on to his, while the other clenched a block of wood Bessa had given to her. It had a woman and child painted on it, and on the back of the block in Bessa's handing writing read *My Little Angel and Me.*

Travis, Nora's boyfriend of nine years, cleaned and organized the trays and trays of funeral food brought by Bessa's friends. His brightly colored button-down matched the plum scarf Nora wore on her neck to give her denim midi-dress the flair her mom requested.

Alex joined Travis and placed her hand on his arm. "Leave it. It'll wait."

Nora's voice traveled from the other room, "He can't let it. Let him clean. It will give him something to do. He can't sit idle. He's like a car ready to race, his engine revving at a stop light until it's put into gear."

"Vroom, vroom." Travis combined meat and cheese trays, ignoring Alex's request.

"I've trained him well," Nora said. Nora and Travis were in their ninth year together. They both had impressive jobs in the financial world and no desire to get married or have kids–so they said.

Bessa had thought differently and shared those thoughts with Alex one night after the family gathered for another so called *Could be* The Last Supper. "Do you see the way Nora looks at Letti?" Bessa had asked Alex. "I don't care what they say, they'll have babies."

"Do you think Travis wants kids?" Alex had asked Bessa.

"Travis loves my daughter. He'll do whatever she wants."

Alex's stomach turned, which brought her back to the gathering. Realizing she hadn't eaten, Alex went to the refrigerator and found the deviled eggs she had stashed in the back after seeing them on the table at the beginning of the day. She bit in and chewed slowly. With food still in her mouth, she said, "Oh my god, who made these, they taste like my Mother's, the relish in them," she said, "turmeric and ginger." They reminded her of family gatherings with her mother and father so long ago. Before their divorce, before her mother moved back to England.

The silence in the room broke her second of contentment. *Bessa wouldn't want us to be like this*, Alex thought. She held up the envelopes the priest gave her. "I have letters."

The three siblings looked up. Letti's little body stayed limp in her Uncle Jens' lap.

Alex held out her hands. "I can take her to her room."

Letti sighed.

Jens tightened his hold. "I'd rather keep her, if that's okay."

Alex chuckled. "She's got you wrapped." Jens, unlike his brother Lukas, drifted in and out of relationships. Letti was the only female, besides Bessa, he caved to. According to Jens, Letti could do no wrong, and she knew it.

Alex sat on the ottoman and faced the siblings, showing them the front of the envelope.

Let's Get This Party Started!

Sketched beneath the words were doodles of party hats, confetti and balloons.

"Only Mama would think this is a party." Nora said.

Alex opened the letter and handed the envelope to her. Nora, like their mom, loved to doodle. As Alex read, her voice changed to mimic her mother-in-law—alive, vivid and full of spunk.

Thank God, it's finally over. Really. Did the priest keep that smelly incense away? Oh, wait. That's right, no Mass! Ha! I'm not Catholic. Service only. Unless I converted. Doubt it. You can thank me for that. You didn't have to sit through an hour-long mass. And you didn't have to go out to a burial site and listen to more dull talk of my life and death. Did I tell you, Father Joe kept trying to convince me to bury the ashes? I told him no. He

tried to convert me too. Nice kid. But really, is he even old enough to be a priest? I told him 'no' on the conversion. Not joining Magnus' church. Sorry, didn't mean to bash your father. Is he here with you?

"Hell, to the no." Jens' entire body stiffened. Letti wiggled and scanned the room. Jens rocked back and forth a little. "Shh."

"Your mom obviously feels the same way," Alex said before continuing to read the letter.

If so, Magnus, you need to leave.

He probably isn't, even though he should. For you kids —not me.

Lukas chuckled, "Keep telling yourself that, Mom."

"What do you mean by that?" Jens asked.

Nora slapped Lukas on the arm and then pointed at Jens, but he raised his hand and pointed to Letti.

"Shut it. I want to hear what Mama has to say," Nora said.

"You know, she never stopped loving him," Lukas said.

"Duh, now shut the hell up." Nora said.

"Hell is not a nice word." Letti mumbled.

Lukas let out a heavy sigh. Alex covered her mouth, trying to hold in the laughter.

"Nice, sis." Jens covered Letti's ears.

"Oh, shut up, boys. You two and your grey shirts. Mama wanted everyone to be colorful."

The brothers stood at the same time. While Lukas undid his belt, Jens placed Letti on the couch, then they dropped their pants to show off their tie-dyed boxers.

Nora covered her face. "Oh, God. I didn't need to see that. I will never unsee that."

Alex waved the letter in the air. "Are you all done? Can I continue?"

"Go ahead, but Mom did not have a thing for dad." Jens yanked up his pants.

"Bessa told me she would always love Grandpa," Letti said.

"Ugh." Jens flopped back onto the couch, and Letti climbed back into his lap.

I bet he tried to sneak away from that hag girlfriend of his, but she probably wouldn't let him come. If's she's in my house, there will be a swirling wind happening soon. I will come back and haunt all of you. Except Letti.

"Bessa loves me the mostest," Letti whispered. Her lashes fluttered.

But if she is here. Just so you're aware Nancy, Magnus and I legally remained husband and wife until the day I died. Yep. Take that.

Nora stared at Alex.

"What?" Lukas breathed.

Jens spit. "There is no way in hell."

"Should I go on?" Alex asked.

Lukas nodded, "Might as well. Not sure if it can get any worse."

My most amazing children, you three are the best thing I've ever done. Ever. I can never repay God for the gift He gave me in you. Never, EVER forget that. You three have always been my heart.

"I'm the favorite," Jens raised his hand.

Letti scowled at her uncle and said, "No. I am."

Jens squeezed her tight and kissed her sweet little cheek. "Yes, you are."

The third greatest gift—because Letti is my second gift after you—is that God took me before he took you. Parents should die first, and I did. Yay!

Well, yay for me.

I win.

Now, it is time for you to move on.

Let's see, what to do with this damn urn?

It's pretty, isn't it?

"It's a bit much, Mom," Jens said.

Letti put her little hand on his face. "It's the universe."

Nora stuck her tongue out at Jens. "She told you."

Alex said I should get the pink speckled one.

Alex stopped reading and said, "Bessa and Letti outvoted me."

"What are we going to do with it," Jens asked.

"Can I keep it in my room?" Letti asked.

Lukas blinked over and over. "Wait. They were still married?" he asked.

Nora responded. "I know, right?!"

Jens whispered, "Why would she stay married to that bastard?"

Nora asked Alex, "Does she say anything else about them being married?"

Alex scanned the letter. "Nope."

Letti and I chose the purple one with all the stars. We have better taste. Although, Alex picked a good husband. Be good to her, Lukas. If you don't, well, I will come back. I will haunt you.

Alex winked at her husband. "At least she knows you're a good seed."

I wonder, can I see what you all are doing all the time now? Actually, I don't believe I want that gift. So many things a mother shouldn't see...

Nora pointed to Jens. "You're fu-" Nora's eyes darted toward Letti, then back to Jens, "screwed if mom can see what you're doing."

Okay, back to what to do with me.

"Back to why you're still married to Daddy," Nora said.

I know you wanted to put me in that box we colored. Did you forget about the box? We made it for your grandmother after she died. As I recall, the three of you wanted to know where dead people went.

Jenny Boy, you were so worried about where she would go. Lukas was practical. "A box," he said. Nora wanted to make it pretty. So, we colored a cardboard box for your grandma. She would have loved it. I don't know where that box ever went. Your father probably tossed it. He never liked Mom. That's because she didn't trust him. Things that make you go, hmm. Who used to say that?

"Arsenio Hall," Lukas called out like a contestant on a television game show.

Did we bury her in it? Wouldn't that be cool? I think the Lutherans let you do that sort of thing, but I don't know.

Nora raised her hand. "Don't judge me. I have it."

Jens used his finger to tap on Nora's arm over and over, like a woodpecker digging a hole into a tree. "I'm so judging."

Letti pushed away from her uncle and crawled across her aunt to get to her Daddy.

Anyway, now I'm stuffed in this fabulous glass urn. I'm afraid none of you are ready to let go. I heard all of you. I will respect your wishes—for a little while.

But, since you're not ready to bury my ass,

"Ass is not a nice word," Letti said.

"I know baby girl, sorry," Lukas said.

then I get to do this MY way.

Until you can figure it out, I will spend a year with each of you. Yes, you get to pass me around. We will start in the order you were born.

Lukas, you get me first.

Everyone was aware of Bessa's plan, but saying it out loud made it real.

Alex snickered, "I love my mother-in-law. But I'm not sure how I feel about this now. We're actually going to keep the ashes in the house? Where do I put them? What if they break?" She covered her mouth with her fingertips.

Lucky you!

Here we go. Be nice to me. Don't break me. Alex will never let me hear the end of it. She would have chosen the metal container.

Alex tossed the letter to Lukas. "That's creepy. It's like she can read my mind. Or she's in the house."

"It will be okay, Mommy. She can stay in my room," Letti reassured her.

Alex stood and walked into the kitchen. "Oh, that will be good. I wonder what your teacher will think? Or how the town will talk? I can see it now on the county website, the county newspaper, or one of the social media groups. Hey guys… Larsens let their daughter have an urn in her bedroom. Do you think we should call social services?"

"That's why I don't live in a small town." Nora said.

Lukas read on.

You will receive a letter every year on the Saturday after the anniversary of my funeral or close to it. Yes, my funeral. Not my death. Funerals are ridiculous, so it is fitting you get the letter on that day. It would be awesome if you could gather as a family to pass me along. Try to gather on a weekend when you have time to be together, to talk, listen to each other. Celebrate your lives. And listen to my words of wisdom and/or full-of-shit thoughts.

Letti jumped off her Daddy's lap. "Is Bessa really saying all those bad words?"

I love gatherings.

Laugh today. I would if I could. Actually, I'm confident I'm looking down at all of you and smiling.

Yours for eternity,

Mom/Mama

Alex brought the other letter over to Lukas. "It's for Letti."

Letti jumped up and down. "For me?"

"Just for you." Alex reached down and brushed her cheek with a finger.

"Daddy, will you read it?"

"I'd be honored," Lukas said,

"Nobody talks during my letter," Letti warned the group as she climbed back onto the couch.

Jens gave Letti a miniature salute. Alex sat next to Lukas and scooped up Letti in her lap.

Dear Letti,

My sweet, sweet most precious girl. I love you more than any words.

"I love you too, Bessa," Letti whispered.

More than all the stars in the universe.

"Forever and ever and ever," Letti wrapped her arm around Lukas.

Forever. You are my favorite human being! You are the light of my life! You are my moon and stars. You are my sun. You are my blue sky. You are the sweetest pitter-patter of the rain that helps all the flowers grow.

"Bessa loves the flowers. I always pick her one when we feed the chickens." Letti wiggled. "Will you feed the chickens with me now, Mama?"

"Yes, Letti-girl, I will feed the chickens with you." Alex held onto Letti's hand.

I will miss you the most.

"I miss you most," Letti said.

I believe with all that I am, I will see you again one day. Try to remember me. But when you forget, search your heart, I will always be there.

Take care of my donkeys, Tinkerbell, and Tiger Lily. Tiger Lily loves you best, probably because you just call her Lily.

"I love Lily," Letti said.

Love your Daddy and Mommy. Forgive them always—even when they do silly things. They will do silly things. And sometimes, the silly things will make you mad.

Letti asked Lukas, "Why would silly things make me mad?"

Your daddy has the wonderful gift of being able to forgive. Make sure he doesn't lose it. Make sure he loves and forgives always. Your mama will help you with this because she is the best mommy in the whole entire world.

Remember, life is short. When bad things happen, pretend you're a dog that just pooped; kick dirt over it and move on. Laugh and Live.

Forever,

Your Bessa

Letti slid off Alex's lap and informed the group, "Bessa is funny." Then she kicked her feet back. "I'm gonna kick dirt over the dying. Bessa told me she'd be okay, and I believe her.

2. THIS IS NOT MY CIRCUS

Alex needed tea, the internet, and space away from Lukas who stayed home from work to replace baseboards on the main floor of their house. She didn't want to deal with the nail gun noise and occasional outburst of f-bombs. Once a hotel in the early 1900s, her favorite coffee shop had the rustic feel of a cabin in the mountains. It was a place Alex could sit in a corner and hide; or find a spot by the window and look out at the people strolling down Main Street; or sit at a small table outside and take in the sun; or grab a spot at the bar and talk to the baristas.

Alex waited at the counter inhaling rich espresso beans when the barista blurted out, "Tell your daughter I've decided on cremation. And," she turned up the steam for the milk, "I want some of my ashes buried with my dog under the tree in my parent's backyard."

Alex squinted her eyes and curled her mouth before speaking, "What?"

"She came in with your husband and asked me what I

would do with my ashes when I die," the barista informed Alex. "I had to mull it over."

Alex tilted her head. "I don't know if you can bury ashes in your backyard. I doubt the HOA would approve."

The young woman shrugged her shoulders. "Then I want to donate my organs." She poured the milk into the paper cup and created a perfect cream-colored heart in the liquid. "Especially my heart. Either way, I want them to take my heart."

The guy standing in line behind Alex chimed in, "Can't argue with that." Alex made eye contact, and he must have thought that gave him permission to continue. "When I die, I want my remains taken out to sea. Between Florida and Cuba. I have family in both places. That'd be nice."

What's wrong with people? Does he believe one half his ashes will go south and the other north? Alex gave him a closed mouth grin, paid for her for her tea, and took her cup to the table next to the window. Not that she had room to judge; she wanted her own remains to go to a body farm, so ashes at sea was probably perfectly reasonable. She didn't feel the need to discuss it with strangers.

She connected her earbuds into her computer and then inserted them one at a time into her ears. They weren't playing anything, but it kept people coming in and out of the shop from talking to her when she needed to concentrate. Before she opened the folder with her spreadsheet, she felt a foot softly kick hers. She looked up and saw her father-in-law, Magnus.

Her gaze met his, but her mouth did not mimic his smile. Alex kept her face blank, like a clean piece of white paper without words. It had been over a year since she had seen Magnus in person, even though Lukas and Letti had gone to lunch with him before Bessa died. He seemed shorter and worn. His hair, still the same gray, had thinned. The wrinkles deepened and the elasticity of his skin weakened, causing it to hang. Magnus, never a very muscular man, seemed frail. The blue in his eyes had dulled. *Why didn't Lukas mention this?*

Magnus tugged at his ears.

Alex removed the cord hanging from her right ear. "Can I help you?"

"Wow. I bet you never talked to Jules that way."

"We called her Bessa, and she never warranted it."

Magnus sat next to Alex in the empty chair and peeked out the window.

Alex followed his gaze to the vehicle parked along the street. Nancy, Magnus' longtime girlfriend, sat waiting in the passenger seat. "Better not get caught talking to the enemy," she warned him.

"You're not the enemy."

"Oh, that's right. Your children are."

He slouched. "How are they? How was the funeral?" He clenched his hands together, one thumb on top of another, rubbing it as if he were trying to massage a pain away.

Tired of being the buffer between Magnus and Lukas, Alex grabbed her things and shoved them into her oversized black purse. "I'm not doing this, Magnus. Call your children." At one time, she tried to see both sides, although she never understood how Magnus could leave Bessa, but that was BA, Before Alex.

Magnus placed his head into his palms.

"It's not that hard, Magnus. They are your kids. Flesh and blood. I know Nancy's family takes up a lot of your time, but your kids deserve their father. Just saying." She stood and walked out of the shop. Nancy had two children. A son who didn't talk to her for reasons not shared with the Larsen family. And a daughter, Crissy, who was an addict. Crissy had two kids who were in and out of her life. Nancy did all she could for them, and while Alex admired that part of Nancy, Nancy's ugliness showed more than her kindness, toward the Larsen family.

Alex's first instinct when she exited the building was to take a sharp right turn and take the long way to her car, but she would not tiptoe around for *them*. She glanced into the open window of the car and caught Nancy's eye.

"Alex, dear." Nancy's hand flew up and the car door flung open.

Alex stepped back.

Once out of the car, Nancy smoothed the wrinkles in her pants and straightened her posture before strutting toward Alex. She held out her arms, "Come give Mama Nancy a hug."

Alex stiffened. "Nancy," she said sharply, while clutching her bag.

Nancy tucked her bleached out hair behind her ears. She seemed to age better than Magnus, but her puffy eyes bulged when she spoke, "I'm not mad at you, dear. It's your brother-in-law that needs to learn manners and respect."

One earns respect. Alex clenched her teeth.

"How's my Letti? It's time we all get over all this nonsense and have Christmas at Granny's this year."

She's not your Letti. You're not her granny, not Lukas', Nora's, or Jens' mother, or even stepmother, and I wish you'd just shut it. You and your fake hair, fake boobs, and fake concern. Shut it. Alex wondered if Nancy knew that Magnus and Bessa were still married when she died. Oh, how fun that would be to tell her.

Magnus appeared holding two cups of coffee and joined

in on the conversation like nothing was wrong. "That would be nice."

Alex dug her fingers into her bag. "It's time? What does that mean, Nancy?" She couldn't hold it in any longer.

"Now that Julia's—" Nancy said.

Alex's fingernail sliced into the bag along the smooth plastic of her computer and her nail ripped. "Oh, no, you—"

Magnus interrupted. "I miss the kids. What Nancy is saying is we should be together." He handed Nancy her coffee, "Half caramel, half sugar-free vanilla, skim milk with a dash of cinnamon."

She took a sip and handed it back to him. "I need more cinnamon."

He took the cup. "We should sit down and talk."

Nancy placed her hand on Alex's arm. "That would be lovely. Magnus finally asked me to marry him. Now, I can take my rightful place in this family. Kind of like Camilla after Diana's death."

Alex quivered. Then she hissed back. "No one is taking Bessa's place. And he only asked you to marry him, because he's finally free to do so."

Nancy asked Magnus. "What is she talking about?"

"I'll get the cinnamon," he said.

"What on earth is she talking about?" Nancy flung her arm up which hit Magnus, causing the cup he was holding to fly out of his hand and into the open window of their car onto her seat. Her voice trembled. "Now I can't even sit in my car." She glared at Magnus and then told Alex, "Alex, dear. You must take me home."

Alex laughed. "This is not my circus."

3. ALEXANDRIA CLAIR EDMONDSON WALKER! LARSEN

Alex sat in her compact SUV with the windows rolled up and the air conditioner on high. She looked down into the cupholder, which was empty. "For the love of— Shit. Shit. Shit." She pounded on the steering wheel with her fists. She had forgotten her tea on the table inside the coffee shop and she wasn't about to go back in and get it. Glad she had the windows tinted to the full extent of the law, Alex wondered if the day could get any worse, when her phone rang. The screen read *Mother*.

Margaret Edmondson. Born in the west part of Sussex, England in 1947, was an only child. She graduated in the top of her class in 1965. Against her father's wishes, she continued her education, graduating from university in 1970. She moved to the United States with her best friend Francisca, and that is where she met George Walker, whom she married in 1973. Alex was born in 1975. Margaret and George divorced in 1990 for reasons not shared with Alex until she was twenty. Margaret moved back to London in 1996. This is the story Alex told Letti. Sometimes Letti wanted to know more about her grandmother, who lived on the other side of the pond, but Alex didn't really know Margaret anymore. Nor did she know George, her father, but he wasn't the one calling.

Alex sulked down in her seat and pressed the arrow button to slow the fan blowing on her face before answering. "Hello, Mother."

"Alexandria."

"How are you?"

"Well. I'm doing well. How are you?"

"Good." Sweat trickled from her brow. She knew she messed up.

"Good at what?"

"I'm well. What's up?"

Alex could hear the sigh.

"I'm coming out to Denver in two weeks and staying seven days. I will arrive on June eighth and leave the night of the fourteenth."

Alex switched the phone to speaker, slid it into the holder attached to vent, yanked the leather notebook out of her purse and started scribbling.

Mother 8 - 14

Clean house

Condensed Milk - Good one in a can - Organic!

Baseboards

Tea - Breakfast - Organic

Rings in the toilet - make sure they're gone - pumice - hardware store should have

Ham - the quality stuff from the deli in Lakewood

English muff

"Alexandria? Are you listening?"

"Yes. Sorry. That will be nice." Alex shuffled the pages in her book looking for a clean sheet, and the paper cut through her finger. She stuck it in her mouth and tasted the copper. She didn't have time for this... broken nail, cut finger, crazy in-laws, and Margaret.

Clean guest room

Fancy soap

New towels - Fluffy

Extra toothbrush, razor, face soap

Rose oil!

Candles?

"Wonderful, I will make reservations for dinner and tea. What days are good for you?"

New Dress and shoes for tea

Do I have a damn hat?

"Alexandria?"

"I can make dinner and you can come to the house. We have plenty of room for you to stay."

Salmon - Wild

Rice Wild

Some kind of creamy sauce - not sweet

"That is unnecessary. We've already made reservations at the hotel. What days are good? I will make plans for dinner and tea."

We? Who are we? Is she going to let me into this part of her life? Was she bringing Francisca? "You've never been to the house, Mother. At least come out for dinner."

"That is nice of you, but I'd rather take your family out for a proper meal. Also, it would be delightful to take Scarlett to afternoon tea."

Alex stuck her finger in her mouth and bit at her nail with her teeth. "Mother, that will not work."

"Pardon me?"

"Fancy dinner, afternoon tea. Not going to work. Letti is six." Alex used the nickname given to her daughter, Scarlett.

"When did you stop talking in complete sentences?"

"Mom."

"Mother."

"Fucker." Shit. It just came out.

"Alexandria Clair Edmonson Walker."

"Larsen."

"Call me when you've come to your senses."

Dial tone.

"Shit. Shit. Shit." Alex took her pen and dug X's into the pages.

4. WHAT ABOUT HER GIRLFRIEND?

Letti stood on the wooden step-stool and helped Alex roll out the dough onto the granite island in the kitchen. They were making cabbage rolls, otherwise known as runzas. Lukas had his head stuck in the computer, putting together a bid for cabinets and trim. "Smoked gouda okay?" she asked. He liked cheese in his.

"I'd rather have pepper jack." Lukas said.

"Guess who I saw today?" She asked in a playful tone.

He closed the computer. He was good at what he did, which was a blessing and a curse. Even if the rest of the trade struggled for work, Lukas usually had more work than he knew what to do with. "I give, who did you see?"

"Your dad."

Lukas stood. He moved to the kitchen and sat at the bar stool. "How was your day, Letti?"

Letti pushed her little fingers into the dough. "Good. Adriana's family has a building in Brazil where they put their dead family."

Alex gasped. "Letti, honey. It might not be a good idea to ask your friends about where they put their dead people."

Letti grabbed the roller from Alex. "It's okay. Everyone except Jimmy likes to talk about it."

"Is this ever going to end?" Lukas added the hamburger and cabbage mixture onto the rolled-out dough.

"Your mom started this." She folded the dough over and pinched it closed in the middle. "I saw Nancy, too."

"Don't care."

"I may have let it slip to your father that I knew he was still married to your mom."

"Doesn't matter."

"Your dad looks awful."

"He made his bed."

Alex folded the dough around the meat and pinched it closed, pressing the dough together hard between her fingers. She blurted out, "Speaking of parents, my mother is coming."

Lukas threw up his hands. "There goes the neighborhood."

Letti spun the barrel on the wooden rolling pin. "Does Grandmother like us?"

Alex leaned into her daughter. "Of course she does, why would you ask that?"

"She doesn't come see us, ever."

Alex exhaled and Lukas shrugged his shoulders.

Alex grabbed a piece of dough, kneading it between her palms. "She wants to take you and me to afternoon tea when she comes out."

"Oh, yes! A real tea party?" Letti asked. "Can we get hats? Can we go on the computer and look at hats? Bessa said in England, where Grandmother lives, they wear hats at tea parties."

"Wash your hands first," Lukas said.

Letti's little voice sang in a high pitch as she ran to the

bathroom at the end of the hall. "Yay, yay, yay, we're getting hats. We're going to a tea party."

Alex dropped the dough onto the counter. "At least she's happy."

The last time Margaret Edmonson came to their house, they lived in a cul-de-sac in town. Margaret thought the neighborhood was dumpy, she kept telling Lukas he worked too much; she hated the way Alex decorated the house, and the neighbor across the street annoyed her.

Lukas placed the tray of runzas in the oven and rubbed Alex's shoulders. "Not trying to be a dick, but your Mom—"

Alex cut him off. "I know, I know. I'm sure her coming doesn't make you happy."

He put his hand up. "Can I finish?"

"Sorry."

"Your mother may be a big pain in the ass, but you have her."

"She will hate it here."

"No, she won't."

"Yes, she will."

"It was Bessa's, she won't criticize."

"I bet you a quarter."

"I'd rather have a blow job."

Alex wiped the flour off his cheek. "You wish."

"Yep." He raised his eyebrows.

Letti skipped back into the kitchen and crawled onto the chair next to Lukas' computer. "Ready to look at hats!"

Alex whispered into her husband's ear, "You should call your dad."

Lukas sighed, "I've tried. He doesn't return my calls."

Letti rocked back and forth. "Tell him I miss him."

"What?" Lukas said.

"Tell Grandpa, I miss him." Letti lifted the top of the computer. "Come on, Mommy. Hats."

Alex winked at her husband before sitting next to Letti. Then she entered high tea hats into the search engine and let her daughter scroll through the online store. It didn't take Letti long to figure out what she wanted. "I want the pink one," she said.

"That will be too big for you," Alex said, and then changed the search to kids' high tea hats.

"I don't like those," Letti crossed her arms at the sight of the straw hats. Alex didn't blame her, they were lame. Alex searched until she found fascinator hats with bands, thinking they would pass Letti's scrutiny.

Letti scrunched up her face. "No. That's not a real hat."

Alex went back to the pink hat and found the smallest size she could. She smirked before adding it to the cart.

"You should get this blue floppy hat, Mommy." Letti took a piece of Alex's hair in her fingers and yanked at it. It was something Letti had done since she was a baby.

"Ouch. Stop." Alex pointed to the black cambric bowler. "This one." She added it to the cart.

"What one will Grandmother like?"

"She'll bring her own," Alex said.

"No." Letti said, pointing to a huge white floppy papyrus. "That one."

"I don't think so, honey."

"Why?"

"Your grandmother does not like surprises."

"What about her girlfriend?" Letti asked.

"What?" Alex let go of the computer, then grabbed it before it fell onto the wooden floor. "How do you know about Grandmother's girlfriend?"

Without looking up, Letti informed Alex, "Bessa showed me pictures."

"How did Bessa have pictures?"

"On the computer." Letti opened the computer. "She's not married to her girlfriend like Bessa and Grandpa are, but she loves her girlfriend more than Grandpa loved Bessa. That's what Bessa told me."

"Oh?"

"Did Grandmother love your dad?"

"Um." Alex didn't know how to answer this question. Everyone loved George Walker. Even Margaret still loved George Walker. They had remained friends after the divorce. But unlike Margaret, who remained in contact, George was a man who traveled and only came around every few years. Most of his girlfriends, were either same age or younger than Alex.

Lukas picked up his daughter. "Do you know how much I love you?" He dropped her on the couch and she giggled.

5. GRAMMY FRANNY

Alex held Letti's hand as she stepped off the light rail that took her from the furthest station south to downtown Denver. The sun broke through the clouds that lingered, and city workers planted purple and yellow petunias in the large pots along the street. Letti pointed to the blooms and then touched the skirt of her embroidered cream dress. "Mommy, they match my dress."

"You're beautiful, Letti-girl." Alex said, hoping her own outfit would pass Margaret's scrutiny. Before they left, Lukas went on and on about how beautiful his girls were, but Alex knew she could have worn overalls and he would have said the same.

Letti tugged at the cardigan Alex forced her to put on. "It's hot, do I have to wear this?" It was twenty degrees colder when they walked out their front door where the elevation was 6600 feet.

Alex tried her best to keep out of others' way on the sidewalk. "No. You can take it off, but you have to carry it."

Letti yanked it off and held it in a ball.

Alex extended her hand, and Letti grinned while

handing the sweater over. Alex unrumpled it before folding it in half and handing it back to her. "You're still carrying it."

"You made me bring it," Letti argued.

Alex shot her the mom look and placed the cardigan over Letti's arm. She tugged at her blue and white polka dot wrap dress, wondering if she'd made the right choice about coming. And she was also no longer confident about wearing the floppy blue hat Letti begged her to get. She peeked down at her watch. They had ten minutes to walk to the historic downtown hotel. Right on time, which meant they'd be late according to Margaret's clock.

Letti ran to the entrance of the hotel. "Mommy, spinning doors. Can we go around twice?"

Alex leaned down, so she was eye to eye with her daughter and took a deep breath. "Letti-girl, remember when I said we have to be really, really good and act like we are all grown up?"

Letti nodded, her smile disappearing.

"Grownups don't go around the spinning door twice."

Letti put her hand on her hip. "Uncle Jens does."

"I'm going to tell you a secret." Alex took out a bobby pin from her clutch and attached it to Letti's hat on the side where it dropped. "Uncle Jens is not a real grown up."

Upon entering the building, Alex took in the sweet scent of the soft amber, smoky vanilla, cinnamon, and musk—Shalimar. Mother. Margaret sat on an empty seat across from a silver-plated pedestal drinking fountain. She wore her sleek gray hair in the same bob she had since Alex was young, with her bangs hanging just below her eyebrows. Alex knew her mother's hair had tons of curl, but Margaret wouldn't show that side of herself in public–the side Alex loved when she was a child. Alex longed for the woman who would walk around the house with her hair in a tangled mess. When Margaret let herself be free, it changed her. Somehow her mood relaxed with her hair.

Margaret stood and pressed ever so slightly at her floral plum dress that didn't quite match the hat Letti picked for her. She gleamed when she spoke to Letti. "You're stunning, Scarlett. Turn around." She spun her finger in a circle.

Alex took Letti's finger and helped her twirl.

"Exquisite." Margaret rubbed her hands together and then reached down and hugged Letti. She then stood and nodded at Alex.

I knew I should have gotten the other hat, Alex thought as she yanked at her dress. She kept the space between them, observing Letti and her mother interact.

"Do you like your hat?" Letti asked.

"I adore my hat." Margaret said. Alex had the hats shipped directly to the hotel, knowing her mother would not appreciate having it given to her minutes before tea. Alex had also made sure Margaret was aware Letti had picked them out.

Margaret stepped toward Alex and leaned into hug her. Alex shifted her body toward the Grand Lobby of the Hotel where each table had white teacups, matching saucers, and small vases with pink alstroemerias in them. "Where's Francisca?"

Margaret straightened her back. "She'll be down in a moment."

Letti opened her hand to Margaret. "You're pretty, Grandmother."

She took the child's hand and strode toward the host stand. "What a lovely thing to say. Thank you, Scarlett."

"Mommy only calls me Scarlett when she's mad. And then she says, Scarlett Jean Larsen." Letti said in a firm but sweet tone.

Margaret bent her knees and looked at Letti. "I'm not mad at you. I love your name, it is vibrant and beautiful, like you. Is it okay if I call you Scarlett instead of Letti?"

Letti batted her lashes and nodded.

Alex observed the two from a few steps behind, a little jealous of the love Margaret poured over Letti. Alex pulled at her dress again. She didn't know what was worse, the static cling of the polyester or the way her pantyhose rode up her ass crack. She smirked.

"That's an interesting facial expression, Alex. Would you like to share something?" Margaret asked.

Alex knew her mother would not find the word ass crack humorous. She sighed and said, "It's nice to see the two of you together."

Margaret asked her granddaughter. "How is school, Scarlett?"

"Good," Letti said.

Margaret tightened her face.

Alex sat straight and raised an eyebrow at Margaret. As far as Alex was concerned, Letti could say "good" as much as she wanted. Etiquette training for Alex started early, but she had no intention of starting it with Letti. It was one thing to be polite and another to have a stick up your ass.

Alex touched Letti's hand. "Tell Grandmother what you like best about school."

Letti lit up. "Reading. I love to read. Mommy is reading me Harry Potter. Bessa gave me *all* the books. Have you read Harry Potter?"

A woman approached the table wearing the hat Letti picked for her. Alex stood and held out her hand. "Hello, Francisca."

Francisca brought Alex close and hugged her tight before kissing both of her cheeks. "Alex, call me Franny,

Fran, Francie, anything but Francisca. Please." She leaned down next to Letti, handing her a single yellow rose. "For you, la chica mía." Then she touched her own hat, "I love my hat, did you pick it out yourself?"

With her nose in the flower, eyes big and wide, Letti nodded.

The server came to the table and pulled the Queen Anne chair out for Francisca. "Hello ladies. Have you been here before?"

Francisca took the seat between Margaret and Letti. "Many times."

Alex wondered if they'd been coming to Denver without letting her know. *Get over yourself, Alex, enjoy the moment. Quit worrying about things you can't change.*

"Would you like to order, or do you need some time?" the server asked.

Margaret picked up her menu. "I'd like a few minutes, please."

Alex followed suit and stuck her nose in the leather bonded book. "I'd like some water, please." *What I'd like is a double. Neat.*

Francisca touched Letti's arm. I interrupted, "What were we talking about?"

"Harry Potter," Letti said.

"I love Harry Potter. So does your Grandmother Maggie," Francisca put her hand on top of Margaret's, patting it.

Alex lowered her menu and gave her mother a sideways look. "Maggie?"

"Alexandria, you may not call me Maggie." Margaret peered over her menu.

"I call her Grandmother," Letti said.

"Yes, you do, Scarlett. I love the way you say it." Margaret set her menu on the table.

Letti tilted her head and asked Francisca. "What should I call you?"

"What would you like to call me?" Francisca took Letti's hands in hers.

"Are you my grandma, too?"

Francisca's posture changed, her spine straight, and her chin even. Alex watched Margaret's chest rise and fall as she breathed in and out.

Alex raised her shoulders before looking at Margaret. "Mother?" Before Margaret could respond, Alex alternated her gaze toward Francisca. "I've never had a problem with the two of you, so I don't get why she's being all *secretive*." She held up two fingers as if to quote the word.

"Why are you being *secretive*, Maggie?" Francisca copied the hand gesture.

"Well, um," Margaret said.

Alex let out a snort. She had never seen her mother unable to answer a question.

"Alexandria, that is not very ladylike."

"She makes that noise when something's funny. I don't know what's so funny now." Letti shrugged her shoulders.

Alex saw the pain in her mother's face. She wondered if that pain reached all the way back to Margaret's childhood. But Margaret would never open up, she couldn't handle rejection. Alex wished her mother would let her in. And then Alex did something she never considered before—she gave in.

Alex took her mother's hand. "I'm sorry, Mother. You're always hiding things, and I don't understand why. I'm happy for you. I'm not Grandfather and Gran. I'm not judging. I wouldn't walk away from you. You always taught me not to judge. You love who you love." Alex winked at Francisca. "One can never have enough mamas."

The server appeared. "Ladies, are you ready to order or do you need more time?"

Margaret opened her menu. "We will have The Royal Palace for four."

"No." Francisca touched the server's arm. "We will have the Dom Perignon Tea for Four. Our beautiful Letti here," she leaned toward her, "Will have the cider royal instead of the champagne."

"Wonderful, and what tea would the lovely Letti like?" the server asked her.

"I would like the herbal chai," Letti held her menu, then said, "please." She whispered to Francisca, "we practiced at home."

"Marvelous job." Francisca patted Letti on the back and then told the server. "I would like the same. We'd like a couple of ice cubes in a glass."

Margaret ordered the Pomegranate Green while Alex opted for the Blackcurrant. Mother and daughter shared a quick glance. A knowing look, without words.

Wrinkles on Francisca's forehead appeared. "What are you two up to?"

Alex winked at her mother. "Just ordering tea." According to Margaret's mother, Alex's Gran, Earl Grey was the only tea one should drink. She'd turn her nose up if anyone ordered anything but Earl Grey for afternoon tea. At that moment, Alex remembered there was a little rebel inside Margaret, and she wondered why she had forgotten.

Letti grabbed her napkin and the utensils inside clanged onto the small plate before falling to the ground.

Alex jumped up to pick up the silver, and Margaret placed her hand on top of hers. "It's only silverware."

Francisca took two sugar cubes from the silver cup in the middle of the table and handed one to Letti. Francisca put the other in her own mouth and breathed in. Letti copied her.

Margaret shook her head. "Are you two eating sugar cubes?"

Francisca beamed. "Yes, we are."

Margaret took the miniature tongs, picked up a cube, and dropped it into Alex's hand. "This used to drive Gran crazy, remember?"

A tear fell onto Alex's cheek. "Yes. I remember very well." The pain rose from her body like a hot-air balloon lifting off the ground. Her mom had returned to her. The woman who slipped sugar cubes to her under the table at afternoon tea when Gran wasn't looking, the woman who would make angels in the snow, and roll down hills albeit small ones, was back.

Margaret rubbed the top of Letti's hand and asked, "What are you going to call Francisca? I call her Fran."

Letti spoke with her mouth full of sugar, "Grammy Franny."

6. THE SECOND LETTER. PASS THE URN DAY

On the anniversary of Bessa's funeral, the family gathered at Nora's house. The middle child of Bessa and Magnus. Unlike Alex's home, Nora's was all one color—white. As a software engineer, she worked hard and didn't have time to decorate, except the pale pink in the baby's room. Empty cartons of Chinese food remained in the kitchen, and everyone but Travis and the new baby sat in the living room. He paced up and down the hall, cradling Julia, the newborn child named after Bessa, in his arms.

"She's been fussy all morning," Nora said.

"Because you won't hold her," Travis cooed at his baby girl, who continued to fuss. Travis and Nora had not tied the knot, and they weren't in any hurry to do so. The baby was enough for them at this point in their lives.

"I'm just trying to help you bond with her, because she loves me best." Nora wrinkled her nose.

"Does not," Travis sang.

"Hand her over," Nora said.

"No."

"Ass wipe."

Letti held out her hand. "You owe me a dollar."

Lukas flicked his sister in the arm. "Seriously? Why do you have such a potty mouth?"

"Okay, mom." Nora flicked him back.

Alex interrupted, flashing the manila envelope.

"How long have you had that?" Lukas asked.

"It came last week," Alex answered. "From Gloucester, Massachusetts."

"And you didn't read it?" Lukas asked.

Alex pointed at the return address. "Gloucester. Who do you know in Gloucester, Massachusetts?"

Nora poked at Jens. "Who the hell does Mom know from Massachusetts?"

Jens waved his sister's hand away. "Quit poking at me."

Letti put her hand back out. "Two dollars."

Alex shrugged her shoulders. "It's strange it came from the east coast."

"It's strange you didn't read it," Jens said.

"It was tempting. I hid it in the top drawer of the china cabinet, a place Lukas never looks and a place that wouldn't taunt me."

Alex tore open the envelope. Inside were two more, a purple one for the siblings and a bright pink one for Letti.

She took the purple one to show her audience. It read:

It's Pass the Urn Day!

After taking the letter out, Alex giggled at the doodles of five urns with text written on them. She handed the envelope to Nora who read, "Don't Shake, Don't Break, Keep out of Water, This Side Up, If Lost Call 555-555-5555." Nora asked her brothers. "What the hell is wrong with our mom?"

"Three dollars," Letti said.

"Hell is not a dirty word. It is a place where bad people go," Nora argued.

"Do people who say bad words go there?" Letti asked.

Jens chuckled. "She got you."

Alex winked at Letti. Nora's potty mouth used to bother Alex, especially in front of Letti. But it was Nora's only true fault. Nora, like Bessa, had a fun and easy breeze about her —a contagious energy. She was like getting your first bag of pop rocks every time you saw her. She'd fizz, crack, and pop —leaving you with a burst of sweet cherry or grape on the palate.

Jens, a little shorter and trimmer than Lukas, stood over six feet tall. His chiseled face and intense blue eyes were the best combination of his parents. He pranced to the kitchen and held out his hands to Travis, who placed the baby in them. Within seconds, Baby Julia fell asleep. "We're all in trouble. Those genes were passed down." Jens held on to Julia's tiny little hand.

Travis flopped onto the stiff couch next to Nora. "Your brother sucks."

Before Alex read again, she told Travis, "He used to get Letti to sleep too. Baby whisperer, we called him. Trust me, it's not something to be jealous of. Embrace it. Use him when he's around."

"Wow." Jens cooed at the baby.

Nora leaned over and flicked him. "Poor baby. The womanizer is getting his feelings hurt."

Jens leaned away, "I have your baby. I can wake her up."

"Back to the letter, people," Alex said.

Hello, my most Amazing Children. I hope you all are here and together. If you're not, well they have that Skype thingy. Yes, Lukas, I said thingy—because I can.

"Slam to the perfect brother." Nora leaned into Lukas.

"I'm not perfect," Lukas leaned back.

Alex grinned. "Nope. Not perfect. Close, but not perfect."

Jens rocked the baby. "Gag."

Did you have a good year with me, Lukas, Alex, and my sweetest Letti?

"Alex talks to you, Mom." Lukas said in a child-like voice.

"Ha. What are you doing now?" Alex waved the letter in the air.

"I give you hugs, Bessa," Letti sat up straight. "Mommy helps me, so I don't drop you."

Alex nodded, looking at the urn. "See, I told you we should have gotten the metal container."

Jens leaned down and whispered to Nora and Travis. "Are they talking to a glass jar?"

"Hugging it, too," Travis responded. "But, like Alex would say, you all are not my circus."

Nora pinched her husband in the arm, "Yes, we are, dickhead."

"Four dollars," Letti put her hand back out.

Alex continued reading.

Why on earth would you talk to a glass vase filled with ash and bone particles? I know you're talking to it. That's just not right!

"Right, Mom," Jens said.

With a smirk on her face, Alex informed her brother-in-law, "Now you're talking to it too."

"Am not. I'm talking to the letter." He chuckled at himself and used his finger like he was directing an orchestra. "Which makes me as crazy as you. Go on, please."

I wish I could have put a secret recorder on the urn. Some-

thing that would share the funny things like they did on Candid Camera. Do you remember Candid Camera? Your dad would. Ask him. If you're not talking to him, you'd better start. Life is temporary. I'm proof. I would say living proof, but, you know how that went.

"She has problems," Lukas said.

"Dad has problems," Jens said.

"I talk to Dad." Nora told Lukas and Jens.

"Good for you." Lukas clapped his hands.

"When that hag lets you talk to him." Jens corrected her.

"What's a hag," Letti asked.

"Back to the letter, people." Alex said. Now she would have to explain hag later.

Anyway, they have that Skype thingy you can use if one of you has gone MIA. Although, I'm really hoping you all are together this year. You need each other.

"We are all here, Mama," Nora said.

"Now we're all talking to her," Alex winked.

Travis stood from the couch. "I'm not." He took the baby from Jens and headed back to the nursery. "They're all crazy, my sweet Julia."

I thought writing these would be easy, like I would give you brilliant advice on your life or something. But writing these letters is hard. I want to be with you. I want to know what you are doing. How you all are.

Since Lukas had me for the year, I will share a story about him. Lukas, when you were about three years old, before we moved to the ranch, we lived in a small sub-division in Colorado Springs. I was pregnant with Jens. Your sister was sleeping, and you were playing with the neighbor kids. I went to check on you, because I never trusted that anyone would watch you as well as I did. I was right!

"Is this the bug story?" Jens plopped down next to Nora.

"Hush," Nora smacked him in the arm.

You and the neighbor boy and girl had disappeared. I've never been so scared in my life! After 20 minutes of scouring the neighborhood, which felt like an eternity, you and your friends walked down the path from the greenbelt with your prize. Bugs! Yes, bugs! I was in tears. Your response to my worry, "Geez, Mom, I was just catchin' bugs." Maybe that's why you love the bees so much.

Mr. Independent—actually all of you are. I'm proud of that trait, in all three of you.

I think you should all go find bugs today. Ladybugs. They were your sister's favorite when she was little. Although it might still be too cold for that.

Speaking of your sister, it's your turn, Nora. Travis, you ready for this? Now you can say your mother-in-law stayed with you for an entire year. I don't care if you're married or not. I'm still your mo-in-law!

Travis strolled back into the room just in time to hear that part of the letter, to which he replied. "Nope. Sorry, Bessa. You're not staying with us this year."

Alex informed him. "And now you're talking to the urn."

Travis planted his forehead into his palm and hurried back to the nursery. "Again, I'm out."

"Do you think she'll be mad if we switch?" Jens asked.

"You can't take her to London next year, so you have to take her this year," Nora said.

"But you have the baby. She might want to spend time with the baby," Jens said.

"Last time I checked, a dead person can't spend time with anyone," Lukas said.

"We can always bury her," Nora suggested.

"I'll take her," Jens said without hesitation.

Have a glorious year, kids! I love you all so much!

Yours for eternity,

Mom/Mama

P.S. Have you talked to Magnus about our marriage? Why we didn't get a divorce?

There were reasons. He'll tell you it was money. It wasn't, and he knows it. Are they married yet?

"Daddy ain't marrying that white trash piece of shit," Nora said.

"Five dollars." Letti held out her hand.

"Go ask Uncle Travis to get five dollars from my purse. But be quiet so you don't wake the baby," Nora said.

Letti stood and whispered, "I will tiptoe."

Nora waited until Letti had disappeared before vomiting all her thoughts. "What the hell? What money?"

"Who knows? Who cares?" Lukas said.

"Dad didn't need money," Jens chimed in.

"He probably needs it now. That bitch looks like she got her face lifted," Nora said.

"Did it improve her look?" Jens asked.

"No."

Lukas stood, "Dad's going to do what Dad's going to do."

"He'd like us all to come over for dinner," Nora mumbled, like she'd reverted to a child.

"What are the conditions?" Lukas asked.

Nora paused. "We all have to apologize to Nancy."

"Not happening," Jens said. "Did you find out why Mom and Pops were still married?"

Nora wrung her hands together. "He doesn't want to talk about it."

Jens forced a laugh. "How 'bout you, brother? Did you ask?"

"Don't care."

Nora pleaded with her brothers. "Will you guys please come to dinner? I want Julia to have at least one grandparent."

"I'm not apologizing for anything," Lukas stated.

Letti strutted back into the room, holding onto her five-dollar bill.

"I'm the one who called her the C word," Jens said.

"What is the C word?" Letti asked.

Lukas picked up Letti and swung her in a circle. "Crabby."

ALEX WAS glad to be home. The day was long, and it drained her. All she wanted to do was lie down and sleep. She stood outside Letti's room. Her walls were painted bright pink with a white wainscoting that made the room bright, especially when the sun peeked in. She had two windows, one facing the north and the other east. If Alex forgot to pull the blackout curtains on the east side, Letti was up with the sun.

Alex couldn't believe Bessa had been gone for a year. While Lukas read the letter from Bessa to Letti, Letti held onto the envelope that Bessa filled with sketched hearts of all sizes and colors.

Dear Letti,

My sweet most precious girl. It's hard to say how old you are. I will assume 7. If I'm wrong, I'm sorry.

"How do you think she knew, Daddy?"

"Bessa was smart. She knew lots of things." Lukas kissed the top of her head.

"Like you, Daddy."

"She knew more."

Little girls always want to be older than they really are. But

when you get older, you'll want to be younger. What are you doing these days?

Alex listened to Letti answering all the questions as if Bessa was in the room. "I'm in third grade, my teacher is Mrs. Christianson. I love reading the most but I'm really good at math and my best friend is Danille, she is funny and likes to dance. I like to dance, too."

How are my donkeys?

"They're good. I make sure they don't eat too much." Letti wrapped her arms through Lukas'. "Daddy helps me clean their feet. I clean up the poop every day and make sure they have clean water."

Do you still love them?

"So much. Lily is still my favorite. But Tink is so sweet. She likes Daddy best."

I bet you do. I knew I could count on you to take care of them. Do you like boys yet?

"No." Letti paused and then tilted it to the side. "Except, Dylan Hanson. He moved into the house on the next street. In the house everyone moves into and then moves out. I hope he stays. He likes the donkeys too. And Lily likes him back. I think since Lily likes him, I can like him. Plus, he's not scared of the bees. All my other friends are scared of the bees—like Mommy."

Alex snorted.

Letti asked Alex, "Wanna come sit with us, Mommy?"

Alex admired the bond between father and daughter. "No thank you, baby."

Letti leaned closer to Lukas.

I will tell you a secret.

Boys are dumb.

Letti took her arms out of Lukas' and raised her left eyebrow.

Except for your daddy.

Letti's shoulders relaxed, and Lukas continued to read.

Your daddy is not dumb. He's the smartest boy I know. I promise you, your daddy will always have your back. So, when you get older and he makes you mad, read this letter again and try to listen to my words.

"My daddy won't make me mad." Letti said.

The day you were born, he cried.

"Why did you cry, Daddy?"

"Because I was so happy." Lukas paused. His eyes met Alex's.

Alex remembered the day as if it were yesterday. It was the day Alex knew she'd picked the right guy to spend her life with.

He said you were a gift from heaven and that he would spend his entire life trying to repay God for his perfect gift. I've never forgotten his words as he held you.

Can you do me a favor today? Can you make sure everyone looks for bugs today?

"Yes," Letti said.

Good girl!

I love you so much!

Forever,

Your Bessa

"We didn't look for bugs today." Letti slid under the covers.

"Tomorrow," Lukas said. "I promise, tomorrow."

After tucking Letti in, Alex and Lukas retreated to their room. "I miss her so much." Lukas could barely get the words out.

"Me too."

"We all needed more time."

“I’m going to say something, and I don’t want you to get mad at me.”

Lukas pulled off his shirt. “Why would I get mad?”

“You should make up with your dad.”

Lukas marched toward the bathroom. “Not up for discussion.” He closed the door.

7. HOG'S ANAL GLAND

Alex and Lukas played grownup and met Jens and his fling of the week for dinner. They sat at the bar in the Italian restaurant on Larimer Square with their drinks, holding hands, waiting for Jens to arrive. Lukas in his pressed jeans and button-down plaid shirt smelled yummy and rugged at the same time. Alex started off with a sundress but the warmth of spring had not yet arrived so she decided to add a ribbed knit jersey with her black boots. A live jazz band played music and Lukas tapped his foot.

It had been almost three weeks since the reading of the second letter from Bessa. Alex hadn't pushed, but she wanted to help the family be whole again. Bessa had wanted that. "Have you talked to your dad lately?"

Lukas let go of Alex's hand and took a swig from his beer. "Can we not do this tonight?"

She placed her arm through his and leaned her head into his shoulder. "You'd be mad if someone called me that." Alex was referring to the word he had used when he last spoke of Nancy, his father's girlfriend.

"Yes, but I wasn't the one who called her that. And besides, you're perfect." Lukas put his hand on her thigh. "Nobody would ever call you that word."

"Hardly." Alex glanced at her watch.

"As usual, he's late." Lukas said.

"It's okay. I'm calculating time to see if I can have another drink."

"Of course you are."

Her limit was two glasses of wine within a four-hour period. Their trip on the light rail would take an hour south to get them back to their car for the following forty minute drive back to the ranch. She assumed dinner wouldn't take over two hours. And she wanted a glass with dinner. "You can be the DD," she said, taking the last sip from her glass.

"It's not my turn." He raised his empty glass at the bartender.

"Would the lady like another cabernet?" the bartender asked.

Alex tapped her fingers on the bottom of her glass. "No, thank you."

Lukas pushed it forward. "She'd love one." Lukas whispered in her ear, "We can always stay the night downtown. Could be fun."

She inhaled the citrus and sandalwood coming from his rough skin, then nodded at the bartender. "I'd love one."

Lukas linked his pinky finger in hers. "Did I tell you, you look amazing tonight?"

"Only half a dozen times." The heat rose in her face. Lukas had a way of making her feel like she was the center of the universe and not only his universe. She took a sip of her wine. "I'd love to stay for the night. Although, I didn't bring anything to sleep in," she said playfully.

Jens arrived at the bar alone. "You two clean up nice," he

said, putting his arm around Lukas. They shook hands and hugged.

Lukas pushed Jens back and gawked. “What’s up with the holes in the jeans?”

Jens slapped his pants like he was pushing dirt off them. “They’re frayed.”

“You’re frayed and a bitch. And the leather jacket is tight, don’t you think?”

Jens slapped Lukas’ stomach. “Jealous, tubby old man?”

Alex peered behind Jens. “Did your date ditch you already?”

Jens ran his fingers through his hair. “She’s in the ladies’ room.” He kissed Alex on the cheek before moving closer to the bar to order for himself and his date. “Double Absolut on the rocks, no lemon and a glass of white zinfandel, please.”

Alex picked up her glass of wine and took a long sip. She understood what fruity white wine meant. Jens’ date probably wasn’t old enough to drink. So much for their grown up night out on the town.

After Jens paid his tab, he picked up his vodka and used it to point at the busty, dark-haired, young woman standing by the host stand. “Desiree is checking on our table.”

Lukas pulled out his wallet. “I’ll close our tab and catch up.”

Alex slid off the barstool like a kid who didn’t want to go to bed and followed Jens, wishing she and Lucas had just gone out by themselves.

When they reached Jens’ date, the girl leaned in to hug Alex. “Hi, I’m Desiree. You must be Alex. Jens talks about you all the time.”

Alex gripped onto her wine and extended her other hand. “It’s so nice to meet you, Desiree. Love your dress.”

"Thank you." Desiree smoothed the side of the chiffon outfit that barely covered her ass.

When they reached the table, Jens sat the glass of blush wine in front of Desiree. "Here you go, babe."

She grabbed his hand, pulling him down next to her. "Thanks, babe." Then she kissed him—open mouthed.

Alex downed the rest of her wine. She didn't need to see this. She wasn't the competition. Besides, Alex was aware she had the prize of the family. Jens called all of his dates babe so he wouldn't confuse their names. Alex felt sorry for Desiree. They wouldn't last more than a couple of months.

Lukas sauntered to the table, carrying his bottle of beer in one hand and Alex's clutch in the other. He placed his stout on the table. "Does it match my shoes?" He put the purse close to his chest before handing it to Alex.

"Thank you, Lukas." Alex set the bag next to her glass of wine.

Lukas held out his hand. "You must be...?"

"Desiree." She licked her lips and held out her hand like he should kiss the top of it.

None of this bothered Alex. It happened all the time. With women on the street and many of Jens dates. If anything, it made her head swell a bit, knowing Lukas was hers. All hers.

Lukas grasped Desiree's hand and shook it like they'd been friends forever, guy friends. "Nice to meet you." He sat down next to Alex and scooted his chair closer to her and rested his hand on her thigh.

A hunky Italian guy appeared. "Looks like you all have drinks," he set the wine menu between the men, while letting his gaze linger on Desiree's boobs. "But I'll leave this for you to browse through. We have some wonderful bottles of red, and a charming blush," he winked at

Desiree. "Can I start you with an appetizer? Calamari, bruschetta?"

"I would love some calamari," Alex said.

Lukas scanned his menu. "Do you have that tasty artichoke dip?"

"The best, made fresh daily. Anything else?"

Jens squinted at the menu.

Lukas pulled his reading glasses from his shirt pocket and slid them across the table.

Jens ignored the gesture. "Anyone want oysters?"

"No," Alex said, curling her lip and scrunching her nose.

"I'll split them with you," Lukas said.

Attempting to learn the age of Jens' date, Alex made small talk. "So, Desiree, what do you do?"

"I model. And act."

"That's exciting. I've never met anyone famous."

Jens scowled at Alex. "Rude."

"Calm down, princess. I wasn't being rude." Alex lifted her glass toward Desiree. "She's gorgeous, why wouldn't she be famous?" Alex set down her glass and gave her brother-in-law a wide-eyed stare.

Desiree blushed and said, "I'm moving to LA in a few months and will take some acting classes and I'm going to dental hygienist school."

"Good to have a back-up plan," Lukas took the readers off the table and put them on before opening the menu again.

Desiree leaned closer to Jens. "I just need to get Jens to come with me. Right, babe?"

Jens put his hand under the table. "Babe, you know I can't. I have work here and I'm moving to London next year."

She pouted. "London's so far away."

Alex picked up the wine list. “Should we order a bottle?”

Desiree smiled, “I’d love a bottle as long as its sweet.”

Alex handed the menu to Jens. “I’ll order another glass. I like my wine dry.”

“Like this music?” Desiree said and then put her head on Jens’ shoulder, “Maybe we can go to a club after?”

The food appeared on the table in waves, with the appetizers first. Lukas took a lemon and squirted a bit of the juice onto the meat before slurping the raw mollusks into his mouth and chewing. Jens did the same, only he put a dab of cocktail sauce on his.

Alex looked away, and Desiree covered her mouth. Desiree dipped a small piece of calamari into a lemony sauce. “I’ll try some of this.”

As the breaded appetizer fell into her mouth Jens informed her, “That’s fried squid you’re eating.”

Lukas picked up a piece of the calamari. “Could be a pig’s ass. I heard some restaurants were substituting hogs’ anal glands and calling it squid.”

Desiree grabbed her napkin, covered her mouth, stood, and ran to bathroom.

Alex snorted and slapped her husband on the arm. “Not nice.”

“Asshole.” Jens dipped a piece of calamari into the sauce and popped it into his mouth.

“Ever thought of dating someone your own age?” Lukas asked.

“Women my age are…” Jens rested his elbow on the table and tapped his index finger on his lips.

Alex picked up her fork like it was a weapon. “I’d be very careful if I were you.”

Lukas scanned the room and leaned in. “I want to know how she’ll be a dental hygienist with all that.” He moved his hands around in a circular motion close to his chest.

Jens smiled. "She has a nice rack, doesn't she?"

"You are a hog's anal gland." Alex stood, tossed her napkin at Jens and went to check on Desiree.

Alex passed Desiree on the way to the restroom. She was talking to the waiter. Desiree looked up in time to see Alex as she placed the phone into the waiter's palm. Alex hustled into the bathroom. She honestly didn't care about the girl and Jens. It was a game her brother-in-law played. The two of them deserved each other. Although Bessa wanted more for her son and had asked Alex to keep an eye out for him. Before returning to the table, Alex looked at the ceiling. "Talk to the man upstairs. I don't think there's any hope for that son of yours."

After taking a slice, Lukas passed the basket of warm bread with a perfect crust that Desiree wouldn't eat. "Too many carbs," she said, passing it to Jens, who took two pieces.

"Babe, you don't know what you're missing."

Desiree ate the salad minus the homemade Italian dressing everyone else drizzled heavily onto the greens. She instead asked for a fresh lemon, which she squeezed and ended up squirting Jens in the face. "Oops. I can kiss that off for you."

When Lukas ordered his meal, Desiree asked, "What's veal."

"Young cattle," he replied.

"You're going to eat baby cows?"

"With a fork," he said. "So tender you don't need a knife."

Alex kicked his shin.

"What?" he asked his wife.

"Stop," she said.

Lukas took another piece of bread and loaded it with butter. "How's it going with Mom?" he asked Jens.

Desiree touched the base of her neck. "I thought your mom passed away?"

"She did," Lukas paused. "We're passing her remains around from house to house, and Jens has her this year." He sat straight and smirked at his brother. "What the hell? Who keeps kicking me?"

Alex put her hand over her mouth, trying to hold back the laughter. "If only Bessa were here now."

Desiree asked, "Who's Bessa?" She squeezed her eyes shut. "Wait, you have your dead mom in your penthouse?"

"Penthouse?" Alex squinted. "Did you move?"

"Nope." Jens said.

Desiree giggled. "I call it the penthouse because he's on the top floor and has access to the roof." She took a sip of her wine and then asked Jens, "Where's is your mom?"

"You can't miss her, she's in a purple glass vase," Lukas said.

Desiree coughed up her drink. She grabbed a napkin and covered her face. "I touched it." She removed herself from the table, again.

Lukas took another bite of his bread and spoke with his mouth full. "How old is she?"

"She's legal," Jens said.

"To drink?" Alex asked.

Jens cocked his head to the side. "Well..."

"Yep, a hog's anal gland." Alex smacked him on the arm with her napkin.

After a few minutes, Desiree appeared, and on her arm was Alex's father.

George Walker was an attractive man. His sixty-six years

on this earth didn't show. He worked out every day, ate well, and drank little. "Look what I found." He pulled out Desiree's chair for her.

Jens stood and held out his hand. "Trying to steal my girl?"

George took his hand and shook it. "If I wanted to steal your girl, I'd have her."

Lukas stood. "George. Let me get you a chair. Join us."

George's gaze found Alex, he beamed. "Lexi, my girl." He held out his arms. He was the only one to call her this. It started when she was born. He didn't like the name Alexandria, and he wasn't about to call her Alex like everyone else. "Alex is a boy's name," he had said.

Alex stood. "Daddy."

Desiree choked. "He's your dad?"

Alex kissed George on the cheek. "The one and only. When did you get into town? Were you going to call?"

"Lexi-girl, I'm only here for a day." He scanned the room. "I'd love to stay and chat, but I have a..."

A woman, supposedly her father's age, stood in the corner. She waved at George. He waved back. He kissed Alex on the cheek. "Tell your mother I said hello."

He left the table.

Alex watched him wander away. "The true hog's anal gland."

8. SPACESHIPS OR GEORGIA O'KEEFFE

Alex drove up to the valet station at the hotel in the plaza. Tired from driving to New Mexico alone, she only wanted to find her room and crash. Alex loved Santa Fe, Lukas didn't. And, although Alex looked forward to the time with her mother and Fran, the rumbling of her stomach wasn't from hunger. It had been a long time since she spent time alone with Margaret. And, until last year's visit, she'd never spent time with Fran and Margaret as a couple.

Alex thought about bringing Letti, but Lukas talked her into going by herself. "It will be good for you to be alone with your mother, and you need a girls' weekend," he had said. She tried to argue, but he promised Letti a day at the amusement park, so Alex lost out.

Margaret reserved two rooms at the hotel. Alex entered her room and found a king-size bed with a yellow hand-painted headboard covered in turquoise flowers scattered off a green vine, a fireplace she wouldn't need, and a balcony with a view of the square, full of life, joy, and music. She opened the door to enjoy the noise outside and then plopped in the middle of the bed. While she loved the quiet of where she lived, the sound of the tourists in the square rocked her to sleep.

AFTER SEVEN FULL hours of uninterrupted comatose bliss, Alex sat on the balcony in her cotton pajamas and the fluffy white robe she found hanging in the bathroom. She watched the world wake, along with the sun rising. The call of chickadees calmed her. Her grandmother on her father's side loved them. Alex had adored her Grandma Walker, and she felt like she was where she should to be in life when she heard the birds chirping.

The sliding door on the balcony next to hers opened. Margaret appeared, fully dressed.

Alex gasped, put her hand on her chest and said. "Va-va-voom." Margaret had let her bangs grow out, and she set her curls free.

Margaret held two mugs. "Good morning Alexandria, would you like some tea?" She passed the cup over to her and blushed. "Fran likes the curls."

Alex took the cup from her mother. "Good morning, Maggie. I would love tea, thank you. And I love the curls, too."

"Must you?" she scolded Alex.

"Must I what?"

"Call me Maggie."

"I must." Alex took a sip of the warm liquid. "Mummy, you make the best tea."

Margaret sighed. "You haven't called me Mummy in ages."

"We haven't done many things in ages." Alex noticed her mother held the mug the same way she did, with two hands, pinky under the handle, middle and ring finger through it, and their index fingers resting on top.

"What is the plan for today?" Margaret asked.

"Things haven't changed that much, Maggie. I'm sure you've written up an agenda." Alex gave her a sideways glance and winked.

"Well." Margaret set the cup on the table, rubbed her hands together, then walked back into her room. "I've composed a list of suggestions."

"No, you don't, Maggie," Fran called out from inside the room. "You're not dictating this trip."

Alex leaned over the wall that separated them. "I told her she could."

"Not my part of it." Fran stuck her towel-covered head out of the sliding glass door of their room and stepped onto their patio. "Wow, it's beautiful out here. I may just sit out here all day. But you know what I'd enjoy more?"

Margaret pushed past Fran with her leather planner in hand. "We will not drive to where they claim the aliens landed."

Alex examined the book that resembled her own. Alex found it funny how over the years she did everything to try to not be her mother, yet in so many ways she was like her. And it was okay.

"Roswell's only three hours away," Fran said.

"I've never been there. Come on, Maggie." Alex raised her eyebrows. "We should do it."

Margaret peered over her reading glasses. "While the two of you chase spaceships, I can visit the Georgia O'Keeffe Museum."

"Not without me." Alex leaned over the railing.

"Count me out." Fran sat in the lounge chair and put her head back. "She always has to go there. Nothing changes.

Same pictures, nothing new. O'Keeffe is dead." She sat up, took out her phone from the pocket in her robe. "I wonder what she did with her body?"

Margaret rolled her eyes. "Speaking of where your dead people are, how is the urn?"

"She's with Jens this year," Alex said.

"I thought it was Nora's turn?" Margaret questioned.

"Are you keeping track of the urn?" Alex asked.

Margaret waved her off. "No. You told me."

Alex thought back, sure she didn't, but it didn't matter.

Fran read from her phone, "Her ashes are scattered on the land around the Ghost Ranch. We should go there."

"No," Margaret and Alex said at the same time.

THEY STROLLED past the local library and Margaret tugged on Alex's arm. She pointed at the entrance. "Fran cannot pass a public library without dropping in. She must check to see if her books are on the shelf." Fran wrote thrillers, which Alex loved reading.

While Fran checked out the shelves, Margaret and Alex sat on a bench in front of a cottonwood tree that had seen better days. The tree resembled an old man ready to leave this world, its once rough skin falling off.

A woman scrolling through her phone while her four children, with distinct shades of red in their hair, played on the grass area. When the woman made eye contact, Margaret smiled at her. "It's nice you bring them to the library."

The woman sighed, paying more attention to her phone than her children. "I wish I had time to check out a book for me, let alone read."

Margaret tilted her head and said, "I think you can use

your phone to put books on hold and then pick them up, can't you? You seem to know how to work those things." Margaret said in that disapproving tone.

The woman looked over and then back at her phone. "I'll have to check on that."

Margaret patted Alex on the leg. "Don't you put library books on hold with your phone for you and Scarlett?"

Alex shook her head. She knew what her mother was up to. "I do, *Maggie*. I do it all the time."

"Maybe you can show this nice young lady how to get online and put books on hold?" Margaret paused. "Reading takes you away from the world and is a gift. A gift parents should pass on to their children."

The woman scooted further away from them. "I'm tech savvy, I can figure it out."

Fran exited the building. "Five out of eight copies of my books are on the shelf."

Margaret lifted her head toward Fran. "She's a New York Times Best-Selling Author, FG Ruiz. Best thrillers out there. You should check out one of her books."

The woman stood. "Thank you." She snapped at her children, "Come on, kids."

"What did you do?" Fran asked.

9. THE THIRD LETTER. YOUR BROTHER, THE INCOMPETENT ONE, LOST THE URN

Sitting on the couch with her tea, looking out at the enormous pine trees swaying in the wind in her backyard, Alex wished she was back in Santa Fe. Alex dialed her mother on Skype. She still found it odd Margaret had become her person.

"Good afternoon, Alexandria," Margaret said. It was 1:24 in London.

"Good morning, Maggie. Why aren't you showing your face?" In Rowley, Colorado, it was 6:24.

"I've applied a face mask and I'm hideous at the moment."

"I can handle it, Maggie."

"I'd rather you not see it. And that's quite enough with the Maggie references."

"Wait, is it that slimy thing you used to goop on your face when I was little?"

"Yes."

"In that case, I appreciate the black screen. What's in it, anyway? It resembles... I can't even say. I'd puke if I said it.

Thinking about it makes me want to vomit. Never mind, I'll pass on the ingredient list."

"You are being dramatic, Alexandria. How is my granddaughter?"

"She finished reading The Secret Garden and I'm sure you'll be receiving a call with a full update on how she loves it and how she wants to grow roses."

"Lovely."

"I hate roses."

"You don't have to like them, Alexandria. There are things a parent should do for their children, regardless." Margaret paused. "I did not do this and I apologize. You, however, do wonderful things for your daughter. I would suggest you get roses and plant them with Scarlett. Can you grow carnations there?"

"Yes, but they won't last."

"Plant them anyway, they smell lovely."

"How's Fran?"

"She's in Scotland, doing research."

"I love her new book, she has recipes in it. Did I tell you I made her bread pudding? Lukas loved it."

"You always were a splendid cook."

"Thank you, Maggie."

"Isn't today the passing of the urn?"

Alex paused before answering, "Yes."

"What's wrong," Margaret asked.

"Jens lost the urn."

Margaret gasped.

ALEX AND LUKAS invited Nora over, even though Jens and the urn weren't coming. Nora was six months pregnant. She scanned the room. "Is everyone well?"

"Nobody's sick here, Nora." Alex handed her a small glass bottle of tea tree oil.

Nora put her palm straight out. "That shit smells nasty." She pulled a plastic bottle of sanitizer out of her purse, doused her hand with it, and rubbed.

Travis stayed home with Julia, who had the sniffles. Alex wanted to ask Nora if she was contagious since Julia was sick. But she didn't, Nora was Lukas' sibling, not hers. Alex didn't understand the sibling thing since she didn't have any. However, she considered herself the worst mom ever because she wasn't capable of carrying a baby long enough to give Letti a little brother or sister.

She took Nora's sweater and purse, gave her a hug, and did the unthinkable. She didn't stick to the plan. Instead, she said matter-of-factly, "Your brother—the incompetent one; Jens, not Lukas—lost your mother."

"What the fuck?" Nora lifted her hands like she would strangle someone.

Lukas shuffled into the house, maneuvering around his sister. He scratched his head and asked Alex, "You told her, didn't you?"

"How the hell do you lose an urn?" Nora asked.

Lukas squeezed his fists shut and said. "I didn't lose it. Your brother did."

"How?"

"He claims the moving company mistakenly packed the urn with his things and shipped it to London."

"Why didn't he ship Mom himself? Mom wasn't even supposed to go to England."

"I didn't ask."

"You should have asked."

"He said he shipped it. It didn't make it."

"Oh. My. God," Nora said. "Does he have a tracking

number? What a jackass. I swear he's like Dad. Idiot." She hugged Lukas. "At least you're normal. God knows the rest of us aren't."

Alex pulled out her phone and showed Nora the screen. "She's supposedly in Bermuda right now."

"She always wanted to travel more," Lukas said.

Nora slapped him on the arm and stomped into the kitchen. "Not funny. I take back the normal comment."

The three of them agreed to continue on with the tradition. Only this time, they sat at the tall table with bowls of chicken soup in front of them. The cold lingered that year, and Alex had batches of soup stored in the freezer for when the mercury dipped below forty degrees. Alex tossed a handful of jalapeños into her bowl.

"I want some of those, but the damn heartburn is killing me, and they seem to bring it on." Nora surveyed the room. "Where's Letti?"

"She's in the other room Skyping with my mother."

"It's great you and your mom are doing so well."

"Yes. Now you all should fix things with your dad," Alex said.

"Oh, I talked to him last week. For a whole *two minutes*. Big whoopty shit. I heard all about Nancy's daughter."

Lukas grabbed the unopened envelope off the table and handed it to his sister. "Can we not talk about Dad?"

With all of Alex's problems over the years with her parents, she still talked to them. She didn't understand how Lukas and Jens didn't talk to their father for years.

Nora opened the large manila envelope and like the year before, two smaller ones slid out. One purple for the grown children and a pink one for Letti. Nora read the writing on the front of the purple one.

Purgatory?

Underneath she had sketched a building with a sign that read *Library*. Nora showed Alex and Lukas. "Like this is supposed to make sense? Oh, wait. There's shit on the back." She studied it and chuckled before handing it over to Lukas.

He shared the view with Alex. There were three headstones. The first upright and round at the top read, ***Julia Olsen Larsen 1944-???? Loved her Family.*** It had an X through it and read ***BORING*** underneath.

The second stone had angels holding the headstone read, ***Julia Olsen Larsen 1944-???? "We're holding her in purgatory until she gets her shit together."***

She shaped the third headstone like a donkey and it read, ***"Don't bury her whole. That's a lot of wasted space burying her into the ground—cremated or not."***

"She knows what she wants. Why doesn't she just tell us?" Lukas put the envelope in the middle of the table.

Nora put down the letter and asked Lukas, "Where is your computer?"

"Office."

"Go get it."

"Why?"

"We need to call your shithead brother." She pulled out her phone and shared out loud the text she sent to Jens.

Nora: Hey jackass, we're calling you on Skype in ten minutes to read the letter. If you don't answer, I will not speak to you ever again.

She faced her phone toward Lukas.

Jens: Fine. Bitchy today?

Nora: Shut the hell up! You lost mom! What does that make you?

"At least he knows what he is." She showed Lukas and Alex his response.

Jens: An idiot.

Lukas left the room. Nora continued sharing the conversation with Alex.

Nora: You said it. I didn't.

Jens: Do you still love me?

Nora: Always. But you're still a jackass.

Nora put down her phone, signed into Skype, and Jens' face flashed across the screen. Before anyone spoke, he said, "I don't want to hear it. I've been on the phone all day with the delivery service."

"Shut up, shithead. I'm reading the letter. You're lucky I let you join us today," Nora said.

Lukas snuck back into the kitchen, put his face in front of the screen, and waved. Then he used his finger to pretend to slit his throat and then pointed at Jens.

"Sit down, you turd." Nora tried to slap Lukas, but missed.

"Did Bessa have family in New York City?" Alex asked.

"No, why?" Nora said.

"The letter was postmarked New York, New York. Last year, Massachusetts. Who is sending these?" Alex asked.

"What's on the front of the letter?" Jens asked.

Nora held the paper close. "Since you lost mom, you can't look at the envelope until you come home. I will save it for you."

Hello, my most AMAZING children! Another year has come and gone. Are you ready to bury my ass yet? What did you do with me for the year, Nora? I bet it took you weeks to even figure out what to do with me.

Nora quit reading. "Shit, am I that predicable? That's all I've been thinking about for the past couple of weeks."

"Just a little," Lukas said.

"Totally," Jens said.

"Jens lost you, Mom. Shut up," Nora scolded him.

Now, don't take that personal. You are the most sane one in the bunch of you three.

Nora's eyes sparkled. "Yep."

You probably brought me into the house, and told Travis, "I can't believe we are doing this."

"Shit. I said that before I left." Nora paused, taking a bite of soup. "Is this chicken breast or thigh meat?"

"Thighs," Alex said.

Nora sighed, "That's why it tastes so good." She put down her spoon and continued to read.

Travis probably tried to put me on the mantel and you probably argued saying, oh, hell no.

"Screw me," Nora pushed the soup toward the center of the table. "He cleared a spot."

Are you still in Colorado? Do you want to be there? Nobody is stopping you from moving back to North Carolina.

"That's not happening, Mama," Nora said.

Make up with Travis' family.

"Not my family to make up with." Nora continued to converse with the letter.

You two—don't hold a grudge for too long. But hold on to what you believe. Nobody says you're obligated to get married and have babies. I love that you two own who you are and are sticking to your life plan.

"Too late. On number two. It's what happens when birth control doesn't work." Nora rubbed her belly.

Alex put her hand on Nora's "Are you okay? We don't have to read this right now." Nora had a life plan. College, marriage, tour Europe, and then get a kick-ass job, and make tons and tons of money.

Nora stood. "I love being a mom. I'm still pissed at my stupid brother." She turned to Lukas. "Not you."

Jens' voice boomed through the computer speaker. "I can hear you."

"Didn't say you couldn't, jerk face."

Nora, you were always the best kid. You made my life so easy, unlike your brothers.

She informed Lukas. "See? Girls are way easier than boys."

"You'll soon find out." Lukas tapped her stomach.

"Could be a girl," Nora said.

"Why didn't you find out?" Lukas asked.

"For the ten-millionth time, we don't want to." She stuck her tongue out at him.

"I think—" Jens said before Nora cut him off.

She put the letter down and pointed at the screen. "You don't get to talk. You get to listen." Then she picked up the letter and continued.

You took two naps a day until you were two, and then you still laid down for one nap until you were four. You loved school. You also loved order. Everything had to be in its place. That may be because the first time you wouldn't clean your room, I grabbed two trash bags and cleaned it for you. While you sat in the bathtub screaming at me, I did a commando run in your room. Before you went to bed, I had you point to a bag you could keep, not allowing you to look in. At the end of the night, I took one bag and took it to the trash. It wasn't the bag you picked. The bag you chose was trash–broken toys and junk. The one I let you keep were your favorite things. I'm the meanest mommy ever. But it got your attention and may be why you're so organized. Your OCD doesn't come from me, though. I hope you are happy. Remember always, our talk before I passed. Just saying.

Nora rubbed her stomach. "She knew I wanted babies. I told her I couldn't start because you and Lukas just..." Her voice trailed off. She studied Alex before saying,. "I felt guilty."

Alex popped up and hugged Nora. "No, no. Never feel guilty for the lives of your babies. They bring me so much joy." Alex touched Nora's stomach.

Nora put her hand on top of Alex's. "Are you mad?"

Alex rubbed Nora's tummy as if she were the Buddha. "Mad as hell. But not at you."

Jens whined. "No, everyone's mad at me."

"Don't flatter yourself, fool." Alex leaned into Nora. "Keep reading."

Okay, next....

Can you imagine Jens taking me for the year?

Lukas chimed in, "Jackass lost you, Mom. Your favorite; lost you."

"Yeah, Mama. Your favorite lost you." Nora repeated.

I want you to introduce me to all the girls you bring home. I don't think this will go over well for you. I can see it now.

Jens brings hot date home.

She sees the shiny vase and says, "Oh, how pretty. Sparkles."

Lukas and Alex started laughing first. Nora joined in and then had a hard time getting through the rest of the letter.

She'd probably be around 20, if you're lucky.

"Nineteen, Mom. Big boobs," Nora said.

"You didn't even meet her," Jens said.

Nora focused on the computer screen. "Okay, were her breasts small?" When Jens didn't respond, Nora repeated herself, "Nineteen, big boobs."

Jens will tell her, 'That's my dead mom.'

She will run out the door. 20-year-olds don't want dead moms hanging around.

"I think she stayed for a bit," Alex said.

"You wouldn't have stayed." Lukas leaned into Alex.

"I'm not stupid." Alex paused. "Although, I continue to be a part of the passing of the urn. And this isn't even my side of the family."

"I've always held that against you." Nora leaned into Alex. "You being able to say these crazy blood lines don't run through yours."

Alex pointed at pictures sitting on the mantel. "Oh, I have my crazy."

Put me in the closet if you want a good sex life.

Note: Wear condoms or keep it dry.

"Thank God Letti's still in the other room." Alex said.

Okay, new subject. What is going on at the library today? When is the last time you all read a book? Go to the library together and pick out a book, then have fun discussing why you chose the book you did. Could be fun...???

"I'm in England, Mom."

"They have libraries there," Lukas said.

"They're all closed. It's almost nine."

I'm tired today. I miss reading. But I'm listening to The Kite Runner. It's a beautiful story. So I leave you today with something I've always told you. Be nice to people. Be nice to each other.

Yours for eternity,

Mom/Mama

Nora sighed, she placed her fingers on the computer and said. "I love you, Jens."

"Love you too, Sissy," Jens said. Then the screen went black.

"Can I have the envelope?" Nora asked.

"Sure," Lukas said.

"I'm sending it to Jens."

. . .

ONCE NORA LEFT, Lukas and Alex sat with Letti, and Lukas read.

Dear Letti,

My sweet most precious girl. You were so little when I left; I bet you are growing so fast.

"I'm the tallest in my class," Letti said.

Remember to always be kind.

Letti nodded her head. "I'm nice to everyone."

You are no better and no worse than anyone.

"What does that mean?" Letti asked Lukas.

"It means everyone is different. But doesn't mean because someone is different than you, they are not as smart as you, or as nice as you, or as good as you."

Letti's scrunched her nose and the little horns appeared on her forehead. "Like Lyza. She's in a wheelchair, but she is really nice, and really smart."

Alex smiled. "Yes, like Lyza. You would never think she's not as good as you."

"She's the smartest girl in the class." Letti said.

There will be mean people in your life, you don't have to pretend to like them, but you don't have to mean to anyone. Remember when we would watch Bambi over and over? Thumper said, "If you can't say something nice..."

"Don't say nothing at all," Letti finished the sentence.

So if you ever feel you will say something you will regret, walk away. Don't speak. I haven't always done this, and there were many times I wish I had.

Letti added, "Mommy says, If you don't have anything nice to say, shut it."

Alex rubbed the top of her head. "Bessa would say that too."

Lukas lifted his brow. "Yep, just like that. Better to not talk to them than to say something you'll regret."

Alex leaned closer to Letti. "Unless you're mad at mommy or daddy, we still want you to talk to us. Broken families hurt."

Letti asked Lukas. "Like how you are broken with Grandpa Magnus?"

Alex gave her husband a sideways look. "Yes. Like Grandpa Magnus."

"You should fix that, Daddy."

What are you reading?

"Mommy is reading me The Chamber of Secrets. It's so good," she squealed.

Have you been going to the Library? Make the old people go to the library today.

"She called you old!" Letti sang to her parents.

Pick out a book. Have you read any of the Spiderwick books? They're one of my favorite.

Soon you will be able to read the Harry Potter books.

Letti's eyes got enormous, and she took a deep breath in. "Did she read them all?"

Lukas handed Alex the letter.

Alex finished reading it, knowing it would make them all sad, but knowing that truth is always better than a lie.

I'm afraid I won't get to the last one, but you will and that makes me happy. Unless you're not reading anymore and that will make me super sad.

Forever,

Your Bessa

10. LIFE, DEATH, AND TOENAILS

Alex made her way off the plane and through the terminal in record time, only to wait thirty minutes for her bags. When all the bags seemed to have dropped, she glanced over at the carousel to her left and noticed her red suitcase circling along with others that spun on the belt waiting for their persons. She pointed to the carousel. "Looks like our bags are over there," she said loud enough for people to hear her, but she didn't wait around to make sure they did; she had to get to the hospital.

After retrieving her luggage, a bus ride to the off-airport parking lot, and the long way to the toll road, she finally exited the highway next to the hospital. Even though the drive to from the airport to home was longer than the drive from the airport to the hospital, Alex felt her blood pressure rising.

Once inside, she raced up the stairs to find Magnus and Nancy alone in the waiting room. She scanned the room and then asked. "Is everything okay?"

"Everything is fine," Nancy said, crossing her arms.

"Where is everyone?"

Nancy moved her head toward the double doors. "The important people got to see the baby."

Alex exhaled. "So she's okay? The baby's okay, too?"

"They named him, Eli. What kind of name is Eli?" Nancy snarled.

"Oh, a boy. How exciting."

Nancy kept yapping. "She named the first one after Julia and then this one, Eli. Not even after Magnus. Is *his* Dad's name Eli?"

Alex started to retaliate and then remembered, if you don't have anything nice to say, SHUT IT. "I will check in with the nurse's station."

"They'll probably let *you* in."

On her way past them, Alex squeezed the top of Magnus' shoulder. "Yes, they probably will." She just couldn't help herself.

Nancy huffed, "Magnus, it's time to go."

THE NURSE TOOK Alex back into the room. Once she entered, she went straight for the sink. Wet, lather, rinse, repeat.

"Six pounds, four ounces," Travis held little Eli.

Alex fixed her gaze at the baby swaddled in a blanket. "He's beautiful." Alex finished drying her hands and glanced around the room. Lukas was talking to someone on his cell phone, "Who's watching Letti and Julia?"

"Hold on to something," Nora said. "Jens."

Alex giggled. The thought of the girls bossing their Uncle Jens around amused her. "When did he get into town?"

"Yesterday."

"Oh, nice."

"You're not worried?" Nora asked.

"No, why?"

"He loses the urn, but you trust him with our daughters?"

Alex sat next to Nora. "Life and Death. Dead and Alive. That urn is not your mom. When she was alive, he cherished every moment with her. He loved and cared for her like nothing I've ever seen. She never wanted for a thing when he was around. He's an ass, but he's a good ass. And the urn wasn't lost; it was late. Big difference." It had showed up three days after their gathering. Nora kept it, wanting Bessa closer to her when the baby came.

"He's *my* brother and I'm not sure *I* trust him."

"Well, if it makes you feel any better, I'll get over to the house and see how things are going."

"You're the best."

"I think I ran your father and Nancy off."

"Now you're double best."

Lukas set his phone on the counter and kissed Alex. "Hey. Jens says the girls are fine."

Alex held out her hands to Travis. "After I hold this sweet child, I'll go pick them up. Julia can stay at our house."

"Take my brother with you," Nora demanded.

"Which one?"

"Both of them. Please."

Alex nuzzled the baby for a few minutes. He was perfect, even with his cone head. His eyes were black and underneath his cap was a full head of dark brown hair, like his father's. Alex breathed in, taking in the smell of life. She pressed her lips on Eli's forehead. "I love you, little one." She placed the baby in Nora's arms.

. . .

Alex and Lukas tried to enter the house, but the doors were locked. Alex tapped on the door. No answer. Lukas rang the bell. No answer. They could hear Letti's laughter coming from out back, so they headed toward the gate. When Alex and Lukas looped around the corner to the back porch, they found Letti with a bottle of bright pink nail polish, painting her Uncle Jens toes.

Lukas pointed to Jens' toes. "Adorable. But it's not your color. No wonder you can't keep a girlfriend."

Jens didn't move. He held onto Julia, who was pulling out credit cards from his wallet. He peered around the toddler and down at Letti. "Keep going. Lookin' good." He looked back at Lukas. "Just because you're not okay with your feminine side doesn't mean I'm not. And chicks dig this. Not that you'd know."

"He'd better not know." Alex flicked her husband.

"Hey, I did nothing." Lukas said.

Julia squirmed away from Jens, forcing him to let her slide to the pavement. She quickly crawled on her knees to Alex, reaching as she got closer. Alex picked her up and kissed her sweet little face.

"You have a perfect little brother," Alex said.

Letti handed the bottle of polish to Jens. "A boy? Ugh."

"I bet your dad wants his done, too," Jens tried to hand the bottle back.

Letti shook her head slowly. "Daddy doesn't do girl things like you."

Lukas patted his brother on the head like he was a well-behaved dog. "And there you have it."

They walked into the house and Jens pointed at the custom-made walnut mantel above the fireplace. "Did she have that made for the urn?"

Lukas placed his hand on his Jens shoulder. "You're not allowed to make fun of Nora. You, the one who lost mom."

"I did not lose mom. Mom is dead."

"You lost the urn."

"The way I see it, she found the way out of the triangle."

"What?" Lukas asked.

"The Bermuda Triangle. She got out."

"You're a dumbass," Lukas said.

"You owe me a dollar, Daddy." Letti said.

"How long are you staying?" Alex asked Jens.

"Two weeks."

Alex made her way down the hall. "I will get some things for Julia, then we can go. Unless you're staying here?"

Jens paused. "I hadn't really thought about it. It's nice and quiet here though."

"Until they bring that newborn home and they are trying to figure out how to manage two children under the age of two." Lukas said.

Jens pushed himself up from the floor. "I'll get my bag."

TWO DAYS LATER, they took Julia back to her parents. When they arrived, they found a handwritten sign on the door:

Baby sleeping. Ring the doorbell and you die. Really. I will kill you with my own two hands. Thank you, An Exhausted Mommy.

The door was unlocked, and Travis was in the kitchen. Alex handed Julia off to him and plopped the diaper bag on the counter. "Where's Nora?"

"Mama?" Julia said.

Travis scooped Julia up and kissed her cheeks. "In our room, nursing. Make sure and wash your hands before you go back there."

Julia squirmed. “Mama. Mama. Mama.”

“Okay, but you have to wash your hands, too.” Travis took Julia to the sink, put soap on her hands, and helped her wash them.

After sanitizing up to her elbows, Alex followed them back. Nora was sitting upright on her bed, cooing at Eli.

“Trade you,” Travis said.

Julia couldn’t get out of his arms fast enough. The exchange was awkward and Alex could see the worry in Nora’s face. “How am I going to do this?”

“When you need help, you’re going to call me. That’s how I’ll get my baby fix.”

“I can’t call you every day.”

“Hell, you can’t. I had your mom every day. I owe someone and it might as well be you.”

“Even with all my crazy?”

“You’re not crazy.”

“Did you wash your hands?”

“Up to here.” Alex touched her elbow. “Both sides.”

“Okay, I guess I can call you.”

11. THE FOURTH LETTER. LET THE GAMES BEGIN!

Lukas, Letti, and Alex drove to Nora's house. It was easier to have gatherings at her house with Julia turning two and Eli, the little walking terror, almost one. Besides, Lukas and Alex's house wasn't baby-proofed. Not for Eli, anyway. Nora and Travis didn't worry about germs anymore. Keeping the snot cleared off Eli's face cured that, but the tissues used to keep him clean, killed several trees daily.

Alex plopped the envelope on the table. "This one came from California. We all know tons of people from California. I'm thinking I'm never going to figure out who is sending these."

"They can all go back, too," Lukas said.

"The letters?" Nora asked.

"No, the Californians."

"You're starting to sound like your father," Alex scolded him.

"I've forgotten what he sounds like, it's been so long since I've talked to him."

"Call him, Lukas." Alex said.

Lukas cursed under his breath. "I spotted five out-of-date license plates yesterday. All from damn California."

"Okay, Mr. Rule Follower. You don't have a tag on that trailer you run around all over town either."

Lukas put his hand on the garage door. "T-Bone the Seventh is back from the slaughterhouse. We brought you some beef. Do you want me to put in in your freezer?"

Nora searched the room. "Seriously? Do you have to say it so loud? Julia loved that cow. Can't you use a different word?"

"Steer."

"I meant for slaughter. Maybe processed. She's not aware you're killing the animals and we're eating them."

"Okay, snowflake."

"Shut the hell up."

Nora placed the computer on the kitchen table. She opened the computer and dialed Jens. "That jackass better answer."

"Two dollars." Letti said.

"Ugh, you little turd." Nora kissed Letti on the check and grabbed money out of her back pocket. "Go check on little Julia. Don't tell her about the cow."

"Steer," Letti corrected her.

When Letti was five, they took over raising the steers. Alex and Lukas agreed that Letti should know the truth and allow her to take an active role in their small ranch. Lukas wanted Letti to understand the sacrifice the animals made for their family. They did their best not to waste any part of the animal. Tripe, the stomach, is not something Alex cooked, but their neighbors loved it and made the best menudo, according to Lukas and Letti. Alex only allowed Lukas to cook the liver when she was out of town, leaving Letti to deal with the smell lingering in the house.

Letti loved the animals, and she came up with naming them all T-Bone. She said it was easier to let them go. Lukas added the numbers at the end of their name.

The screen on the computer was dark, but Jens voice echoed through. "Hang on, I'm naked."

"You'd better be alone, jackass," Nora put her hand between her face and the computer.

"She's leaving now," Jens said.

"Your dick is gonna fall off."

Jens' face appeared. The wall behind him was bare and white. "Nice try. Nobody is here. It's only 7PM."

Alex peeked into the screen and waved. "Are you ever going to decorate?"

"What's the use?" He shrugged his shoulders. "I'll only be here for another nine months tops. Thank God, I miss the sun."

"When are you coming back to Colorado?" Alex asked.

"They're offering me SoCal. If I get San Diego, fine. LA, no."

Nora stood so Jens saw her, "You're just going for the booty."

"She won't talk to me anymore," Jens said.

"I wouldn't either, you're a damn pig," Nora said.

"Your kids will start mimicking you soon and their first word will not be one you like. I hope I'm able to witness what her first curse word will be," he said.

Nora flipped him off and strutted out of sight of the computer camera.

"Okay, let's get this party started," Alex picked up the envelope and hollered, "Lukas, you ready?"

"What's on the envelope?" Jens asked.

Alex lifted it up and turned it toward the computer. "Dominos. Random dominos all over the envelope."

"Does it say anything?"

Let the Games Begin!

On this side of the pond, the three of them sat while Travis managed the three children in the other room. Travis didn't enjoy listening to the letters being read. He confided to Nora that he would rather her tell him about the letter later. He said even though he loved Bessa; he didn't feel the bond like everyone else did.

Alex picked up the letter and looked at Nora, "Do you want to read it?"

She crossed her legs like a kindergartner. "I like to listen."

"And comment," Lukas added.

"Let's get real here, we all like to comment." Nora said.

"Can we hurry this along? I have plans tonight." Jens said.

"Isn't it a little late to go out?" Nora leaned over so she could see Jens in the computer screen.

"For old people like you people." Jens said.

Lukas flicked his fingers at the camera. "My guess is you probably took a nap, and that's the only reason you can still go out."

"Start reading," Jens said.

Okay, that was fun! You all three should have had me for a full year. Did someone bail?

"Jens lost you, Mama." Nora said.

"Everyone knows, for God's sake. Am I ever going to live that one down?" Jens said.

"No," Lukas and Nora said at the same time.

It's okay if one of you did. This is crazy bat shit stuff here. Who puts their damn ashes in a glass urn and asks her children to pass around so they can spend time with her?

"You do, Mom." Lukas said.

I've been asking people what they want done with their bodies when they die. It's kinda funny. Alex wants to her body to go to a body farm.

"Not happening." Lukas told Alex.

Lukas won't do it if she dies first. Better outlive her, Lukas.

Alex gave her husband an enormous grin and winked.

"Still not happening," he scolded her.

Nobody else in this family would tell me what they wanted. I think you all were too afraid to tell me. Like talking about my death would stop it from happening. Didn't work, did it?

"I don't want my remains placed in a jar to sit on a mantel or table of my children every year," Nora said.

The tree thing is cool. Although if you do it on your property, do you have to disclose this when you sell the house? It's not like burying a dog under a tree. Can you imagine coming back to visit the house and asking the new owners if you could go visit your mom because her ashes were under the pine tree out back?

"But passing around an urn is normal." Lukas laughed.

I have a friend whose stepdaughter lives with them and the stepdaughter had her mother's ashes in the closet. That shit wouldn't fly with me. I would flush Nancy's dead bones down the toilet.

"Do you think Daddy will ever marry Nancy?" Nora asked.

"Oh, God, no," Jens said.

Alex paused for a moment, hoping they would talk about it. But the silence in the room told her all she needed to know.

Hey, if your father isn't with that woman anymore, he can take me for the year. He won't do it. Not because of her—well yes, probably because of her—she thinks she rules him and I think that's funny.

But I should keep that crap out of here. He wouldn't keep me because he'd worry I could come out like a genie. And he knows I wouldn't grant him any wishes.

"It would be fun to see Mom come out of the urn and throw down with Dad. Listening as her words slice right through him. She was always good with that," Jens said.

But for you three, I would grant you the world.

I wonder what you'd wish for. Are you happy? I hope you all are happy. I hope you understand how precious life is. How important it is to love the ones you love. Pay attention to them. I see all this technology and it scares me. I hope you turn off the television; I hope you put down your phones; I hope you talk to each other.

I'm sure you wish you could talk to me, I hope you do anyway.

"We all talk to you, Bessa," Alex said.

I hope that I was a good mom. I hope that I was a good grandma.

"The best," Lukas said.

"My role model," Nora said.

Alex took a deep breath, and didn't respond, knowing if she said what she thought, she wouldn't be able to finish the letter. To her, Bessa was as close to perfect as one could get.

Remember, family dinners when you were growing up? Remember when we all shared what the worst thing that happened and then the best thing that happened to each of us that day? I copied that from a movie. A movie where a husband and wife were divorcing. Funny, they got back together in the movie. Anyway, hearing what was your best part of the day—was my favorite part of the day. I hope you pass that on to your kids.

Today I feel like poop, but my favorite part of today was sitting at the table with the three of you playing dominos. I've

always loved just having time with you guys, not having to share you with anyone. Thank you for giving me a little of each of you today. I love you so much.

Yours for eternity,

Mom/Mama

"Worst thing today was I didn't get a nap." Jens paused. "Best thing was hearing your letter."

Nora spoke next. "Worst thing today was, Eli shit up his back and I had to clean it up. Best thing was Eli in the bathtub with Julia playing motorboat with the plastic boats."

Lukas scratched his cheek. "Worst thing was Letti waking me up at five thirty this morning. Best thing was Letti waking me up at five thirty this morning and being able to watch her love on those damn donkeys."

"I'm going to bed, siblings," Jens waved at the screen.

"Wait," Nora said. "Alex didn't share."

Alex answered, "Worst thing, I didn't have evaporated milk for my tea. Best thing, reading this note and seeing the three of you bond."

"Sleep good, old man," Lukas said before shutting down the computer.

LETTI SAT between Lukas and Alex once they arrived home. She no longer waited until bedtime to hear her letter. She held the envelope covered in flower doodles while Lukas read.

My sweet, Letti. What did you do today?

"We went to Auntie Nora's. She's getting married and I get to be a flower girl with Julia. We are doing it at our house. It's going to be so pretty."

What was your favorite part of today? The best thing that happened to you?

"I liked playing with the babies and Uncle Travis. They are so cute. They get very excited when I come over. I wish Mommy could have another baby." Letti leaned her head against Alex.

The emptiness in Alex's stomach jabbed at her. It was like a kick, but her flat stomach didn't move. Lukas kissed the top of Letti's head and said. "But you get all the attention."

"I'd share."

"That's why you're the best only child. Because you're nice and not a brat." Lukas took Alex's pinky in his. Then asked Letti, "Do you want to finish the letter?"

Letti nodded.

Mine was cuddling with you today. And listening to you tell me today, this day, when you were 6, that the best part of your day was when Lily walked over to the fence to get rubs from you. You told me, "I'm not calling her Tiger Lily anymore. She isn't mad like the girl in Peter Pan, she is sweet and happy. Just Lily."

"Just like you," Lukas added.

Forever,

Your Bessa

12. A SPECIAL SEAT FOR THE URN

Alex sat on her deck looking at the barn and the chickens. Her gaze focused to the south, but there was nothing to see. The snow hadn't covered the mountain in months. All that was visible in that direction was smoke. To say it had been dry was an understatement. Although the sunsets were beautiful each night, they came at a price—forest fires that burned for two weeks.

Her cell phone chimed, it was Nora. Alex answered, putting her on speaker. "That stupid bitch is posting crap all over social media. I know she's talking about me." Nora screeched.

Alex muffled the sound in case Letti and Lukas came in from feeding. She listened, once again grateful she didn't let that those sites consume her.

Nora barely took a breath. "All these stupid-ass memes about family ignoring her and all of her Christian posts. If people knew the other side of her. She's has one that reads, 'rising above it all', and another that says something about walking away instead of treating them like they treated you. She needs to practice what she preaches. Honestly, I really don't care anymore. I want her to go away. But NO! She thinks she should be the mother of the bride. She called me last week and asked what color dress she should wear to the wedding?"

"Did you invite her?" Alex asked.

"Hell, no," Nora screamed.

"What did you tell her?"

"I told her it would be a small wedding with only family."

"Oh God, what did she say."

"Something like, well, I am your father's wife. She mumbled something about when they get married. I shut her down. Asked her when the wedding was and the bitch didn't have a date."

"I bet that went over well."

"She made a pfft noise and told me, if she wasn't invited, Daddy wouldn't be coming. I told her that was fine and hung up."

"Did Magnus call you back?"

"He did, but not to apologize for the hag. He left a message to call him back because I didn't answer the phone."

"Did you call him back?"

"No. I'm ignoring them."

"What are you going to do?"

Nora sighed. "Let her come. I want Daddy there. But she will have to sit behind Mama. I'm having a friend make a special seat for the urn."

Dear God.

LUKAS AND ALEX worked on the yard for most of the summer. Because of the heat, the wild flowers weren't bountiful like the previous year, instead most of the grass resembled straw. They started watering the southern part of the property in hopes there would be a few flowers by the time Nora and Travis said I do. Wasting water to promote weed growth and wild flowers wasn't something Lukas agreed on so he concocted a watering system using the gray water from the laundry room to help with conservation. In the end, a few of the white, yellow, and purple wildflowers, along with the reddish orange Indian Paintbrush that were Alex's favorite, sprouted.

Travis and Lukas cleaned out the barn that held tools and tractors so Alex and Nora had room to set up plastic rectangular tables they covered with different colored tablecloths. Nora wanted fun and relaxed, not proper and elegant for her special day. To accomplish that, Nora even took out Bessa's old sewing machine and made the coverings herself from sheets, knowing Bessa would have loved all the colors.

ON THE DAY of the wedding, Blister, a name Travis gave Jens because he would show up after all the hard work, did nothing. For punishment, Nora had Jens hold baby Eli during the ceremony. Whether he could handle the squirming one-year-old, really didn't matter to Nora, she only prayed that the child would need a diaper change when only Jens was around to do it.

The guest list was small. Outside of the sibling group, their father and Nancy, and only close friends with their families, attended. Travis tried to include his family, but when his mother said she would only agree if her pastor baptized Nora, he rescinded the invitation, saying she was baptized as a child. According to Travis' mother, one should be dunked frequently, and she was also concerned that Nora had not been saved. Nora respected their differences in religion and doctrine. She only wished her soon to be mother-in-law would do the same.

Alex peeked out the window of her bathroom and saw most of the attendees seated. Nora chose not to assign seats. Nora purposely had her friends sit in the front rows, which forced Magnus and Nancy to sit in the third row on the right. Alex watched Nancy fidget, looking around, and pointing to the people in front of her. Nancy stood from her seat and plucked Magnus up with her.

Alex slipped back to the bedroom and helped Nora with the flowers in her hair. She didn't need a veil. The flowing cream v-neck wrap dress with kimono sleeves was perfect. Alex stood back and admired Nora's reflection in the mirror she had mounted to her closet door for this day. "You're stunning."

A persistent tap on the bedroom door spooked the two of them. Alex pulled at the bobby-pin in her hand, and told Nora, "Stay put. Don't move."

She walked to the door and cracked it open. Nancy tried to push her way in. "I need to talk to Nora."

Alex stepped into the hall toward Nancy, closing the door behind her. "Hello Nancy. Love your dress."

Nancy tugged at the long gown. "Nora told me to wear gray. She didn't tell me it would be informal." Nancy looked Alex up and down. "But 'the family' is allowed to wear bright pretty clothing. Things need to change, and they need to change now."

"Can you be a sport? Can you find Magnus? It's almost time to have him walk Nora down the aisle."

"He's using the restroom. I need to talk to Nora about the seating chart. I've asked her friends to move and they looked at me like I've got three heads."

Nora flung the door open and poked her head out. "Nancy. There is no damn seating chart. Sit in an open seat. Any one. Pick one."

"But the mother of the bride…"

Nora shook her head. "You. Are. Not. My mother. My mom is the only one with a saved seat."

"She's dead, I'm not."

"We can't have it all, can we?"

"Are you talking about me?"

"I know it's hard for you to believe, but this day isn't about you, Nancy."

Magnus hummed, *Here Comes the Bride* as he advanced down the hall. He halted at the sight of Nora. "You remind me of…" he paused, "the prettiest girl in the world."

"Magnus, we need to talk." Nancy's voice spat venom. She stomped down the hall.

His shoulders sulked, and his face lost the light. "I'll be right back."

Placing her hand on Nora's lower back, Alex guided her inside the bedroom. "Let's finish securing the flowers in your hair." While she pinned the sprig of baby's breath above the wild pink carnations, Alex told her, "Breathe. It's not worth it. This is your day."

"She's going to screw up my day."

"Only if you let her."

"Trust me, she's gonna screw it up."

Someone on the other side of the door tapped softly. "Come in, unless you're Travis," Nora spat.

Magnus opened the door and shuffled in. His face said it all.

Nora glared at him. "What, Daddy? What?"

"After I walk you down the aisle, I will have to go. Nancy is waiting for me in the car."

Nora spun away from her father. “Just go now.”

“I can walk you down the aisle.”

Her voice cracked as she waved him off. “Just go.”

He shuffled out of the room. Alex followed. On the other side of the door, Lukas and Jens stood with their arms crossed. “You might want to find your balls before you leave, Pops,” Jens said, passing him.

Magnus asked Lukas, “What am I supposed to do?”

Lukas put his hand on his father’s shoulder. “If I have to tell you, we’ve really lost you.”

Fifteen minutes later, Julia, Letti, and Alex holding on to baby Eli appeared. Following them, the bride put away the tears and walked between her brothers, arms linked, down the flowered pathway to the altar where the love of her life waited to say, “I do.”

13. THE FIFTH LETTER. BOWLING AND A BIG PLATE OF FRENCH FRIES

With Eli almost two and Julia almost three, it was just easier to continue to meet at Nora's house. Alex thought it might be fun to travel to London, forcing Jens to host, but Margaret was coming to visit, so going to London just to visit the bachelor made little sense.

The manila envelope was postmarked Jacksonville, Florida. Nora printed off a map and circled the states the letters came from, but it was still a mystery who sent them.

On both envelopes were sketches of a bowling lane. Letti's had all ten pins intact, waiting for someone to roll the ball down the lane. The other letter showed the ball hitting the pins with some of them flying in the air.

In their usual positions with the urn sitting in the middle of the table and the computer set up next to it where Jens could see his siblings, Alex read.

Did I ever tell you, your father and I were in a bowling league?

"We haven't talked to Daddy since my wedding, Mama." Nora asked Jens, "Have you talked to him?"

Jens curled his lip. "Yeah, right."

She pushed the computer away and asked Lukas, "You?"

Lukas picked up his phone from the table. "I've texted him a few times."

Alex responded. "He only gets one-word answers." She had more to say, but she didn't want the day to be about Magnus, he didn't deserve it. Alex had ceased pestering her husband to talk to his father.

Did he ever tell you how bad I was? I swear, they stored all my athletic abilities in the three eggs that produced you three kids. Anyway, your dad was so competitive (shocking, right?), it only lasted a year. I wanted to quit in the middle of our league, but I always made you three stick things out, so I made myself finish.

We were having problems that year in our relationship, but believe it or not, the bowling brought us together. We went out once a week without you kids and had our time—Lukas and Alex call them date nights. My favorite part of the night was sharing an enormous plate of french fries at a 24-hour diner in town.

"What is it with her always talking about Pops?" Jens asked.

Nobody answered.

The thing about knowing you're dying is you can cross lines that you could never do before. Oh, I guess I could, and I did, but you all would have given me shit for doing it—and you did. But now you can't. Well, you can, but I won't hear you. I'm six feet under. If you've buried me. Which I doubt.

Lukas shook his head, "No, Mom. You're still being passed around. This last year, you spent with us and now you're going back to Nora because Jens is still in Europe. We've moved you around from room to room, and Alex talks to you daily."

"Do not," Alex argued.

Lukas made a funny face. "Full on conversations." He made circles close to his temple with his index finger.

"I see nothing wrong with that," Nora said.

Lukas spoke to the urn that sat on the mantel. "Letti wanted to take you for show and tell. But since she couldn't, she had five of her friends come to look at you. Now one of them is no longer allowed at our house."

"Really?" Jens hollered.

"Really. Her friend's mom said it must be a weird Catholic thing," Lukas made the sign of the cross.

Alex responded, "I'm sure the church believes we should bury her."

"Did you start going to church?" Jens asked.

Alex peered into the computer. "About as much as you go. But the Catholics like to put their dead in the ground."

Letti entered the room. "You're going to bury Bessa?"

"I still need more turns so don't worry my little nichy, we're not burying her yet," Jens said. Jens started calling Letti nichy after watching an old episode of *Boy Meets World.*

Letti told Nora, "Uncle Travis said he needs help to clean up the baby." Letti pinched her nose. "Eli has poop on his back."

"You tell Uncle Travis, he has poop duty."

"Okay, but can I wait here for a few minutes so I don't smell it?"

Nora pulled Letti onto her lap. "Yep. You can stay here with me. He'll figure it out."

My soul is probably still in purgatory. You all better be praying for me. I might not like it here. Doesn't matter. Death gives me the right to do what I want in these letters at least. I don't care if I'm in trouble.

"Who's in trouble?" Letti asked.

Nora hugged her. "No one. Your Bessa is about to cross lines and we have no choice but to let her."

I'm going to give you relationship advice.

"Uh-oh," Jens said.

The first one is easy, and for all of you. Don't cheat. Period.

Now for Lukas and Alex.

Alex scanned through the document.

"Out loud," Nora said.

If you two ever think about divorcing, I will come back and haunt you.

Letti stood. "Are you getting a divorce?"

Alex took her hand. "No baby, your Daddy and me are never getting a divorce. I love him more than anything."

"More than me?"

"Nope. But close." Alex winked at Lukas.

Nora tugged at Letti. "Sit back down with me."

I'm serious. And although I doubt this will ever happen, relationships are hard, but I would imagine that coming out on the other side of all the yuck is amazing. Not that your relationship is yuck. I just wasn't fortunate enough to come out on the other side of my yuck. However, I was lucky I never had to share my kids. You all took my side and made me first. I would imagine missing out on your dad has taken its toll on all of you, it's probably still happening.

You all should forgive him. I did.

"You would be so damn mad at him now, Mama." Nora shuffled in her seat.

Letti held out her hand, "One dollar."

"Shit. Sorry," Nora said, pulling out money from her jean pocket. "There's two. Keep reading, Alex, before I go broke."

Back to Lukas and Alex. I get so side tracked with your father. Lukas and Alex, can you imagine sharing Letti?

Alex informed Lukas. "I'm not sharing, so you better stay with me."

"Not going anywhere without you, baby."

Nora placed her finger in her mouth. "I'm going to be sick."

It would suck. You two are my favorite couple.

"Aw, we're her favorite." Alex patted her own back.

"Now I'm going to be sick," Jens said.

"You're just jealous," Lukas said.

Letti slid off Nora's lap. "I'm her favorite, people," she said, waving her index finger in the air and heading back down the hall.

I love watching how much you love each other. Talk always.

Nora and Travis.

Alex and asked Nora, "Do you want him to listen to this part of the letter?"

Nora shook her head. "I'll read it to him later. He's changing that shitty diaper. Dammit." She pulled out two more dollars.

Lukas leaned over and peered down the hall. "You can keep it, she didn't hear you."

"Yes, I did." Letti skipped back, grabbed the money, and then disappeared.

Nora and Travis. It's okay to change your mind about what you want in your life. I hope you have babies. I'm going here. The only reason I am is because you both shared with me you felt like you were missing out. I hope you two shared this with each other. If you haven't, now might be the time. Haha!

Alex breathed in. "She would love your babies so much."

Nora held tight to Eli's rag doll monkey. A gift Bessa made for future babies, something Bessa had left with Alex, just in case. She figured they'd have at least three. Alex had a box of things Bessa gave to her to give the kids as they were born. She also crocheted ten blankets.

I'm sad that I won't be there to watch you two grow together. You're both so independent and kind to each other. You will be the best parents, if you choose to be.

Lukas sat next to Nora and took her hand. "They are the best, Mom."

Okay done. Well, one more thing. I had a dream. You had four kids; you were at a park. It was kind of amazing.

"Better get busy," Jens said.

"Shut up, dickhead," Nora said.

Jens.

Alex read the first sentence and then handed Nora the letter for her to read. Alex sat back to listen. "This will be fun."

Find a genuine woman.

Nora laughed. "Yeah, find a real woman, dipshit." She looked back down and then tossed the letter back to Alex. "I'm not reading the rest of this shit."

Alex scanned the letter and could see why. It's not that Nora and Lukas were jealous of their brother, they were, but they weren't. But there was no way Nora would coddle her youngest brother either. They all were aware Jens was the favorite, but they also recognized that he loved Bessa the most.

You are the sweetest of all my children. AND you ALL know it.

"Mama's boy," Lukas mocked him.

You were the only one in the house who noticed when I cut my hair, or colored it, or when I got a new outfit. You brought me flowers all the time. You listened to me. You paid attention. Mama's boy, they all said. If you would treat a woman half as good as you treated me, a genuine woman, dang boy, you'd

have it made. You need to know one thing; you are NOT your father. Once you find her, you will never stray. But don't let the right one pass you by. I think it could have been the girl at the Fleetwood Mac concert. Just saying, Love you, my sweet boy.

"She was hot," Jens said.

"Bessa said she was real. She brought her up every time you dated some bimbo." Alex cringed. "Those were Bessa's words, not mine."

"The one you let get away. Too scared to ask her out." Nora commented.

"Shut it," Jens said.

Nora flipped him off.

You should all go bowling. Yes, go! Eat an enormous plate of fries. Maybe ask your father if he'd like to go with you.

Yours for eternity,

Mom/Mama

After Alex finished reading the letter, she grabbed the box that came to the house and gave it to Nora. "These are for you. From your mom, she's given specific instructions for you to open them with Travis in the room."

"Travis," she yelled.

Nothing.

She picked up her phone and sent him a text. Thirty seconds later, Travis, Letti, Julia, and Eli appeared. Eli's curly hair was wet, and he was in a new outfit.

Inside the box were plaques with a picture of the moon and stars that read, Love You to the Moon and Back, on the bottom left corner of each plaque the kids' names engraved on the wood. Inside was a note. ***"I hoped you'd change your mind. Hug and kiss my grandbabies."***

"Who sent these?" Nora asked, her voice cracking.

Alex shrugged her shoulders. "They came from Florida

with a typed letter to make sure you got them and that you were present for the reading of Letti's letter."

"You brought my letter?" Letti asked.

"Yep." Lukas patted the empty spot next to him.

Letti sat next to him and leaned in to listen.

Nora was caressing the plaque. "How did she know their names?"

Letti scowled at her. "Shh, it's time for my letter."

Dear Letti,

My sweet most precious girl. You're double digits this year! What are you doing? Sports?

"No, I don't really like sports."

Are you still reading?

"Yes. Right now I'm reading Wonder. It's about a boy with an extraordinary face and for the first time he goes to school and the kids make fun of him. I'm almost done. It's very sad and very happy all at the same time. He is very brave."

Are you writing in that diary I sent you?

"Yep. Daddy got me a new one because I wrote on every page."

I was going to send you a new one every year, but what if your Auntie Nora or Uncle Jens blesses you with cousins and they don't get one?

Letti stood and then placed herself between her cousins. "Two. Julia and Eli, they are so cute."

They won't get these letters either. I hope you share the letters. Make copies. Because everything I say to you, I would say to them. It is your job to make sure they will know how much I love them. Only you know how the love of Bessa feels. Promise me you'll tell them.

"I promise, Bessa."

Nora held tightly to the plaques with one hand and wiped her eyes with the other.

How are my girls? Give Lily an extra kiss for me. Did I tell you I went out to see her today, and she put her head on my shoulder. I didn't have a camera to prove it. But I think she finally loves me. Tink got jealous and tried to get in between us, but Lily wouldn't let her. It was so sweet.

Tell the old people to take you (and hopefully your cousins) bowling and order a humongous plate of french fries. Tell them to call Grandpa too. I bet he would love to see you.

I love you and your cousins all the way to the moon and back.

Forever,

Your Bessa

"Can we call Grandpa Magnus?" Letti asked Lukas.

Lukas held up his phone. "I texted him. He said he was busy."

14. HOOK, LINE, AND SINKER

Letti picked out all the hats, although Alex thought Fran may have helped with the decision process as boleros weren't Margaret's style. Alex held onto the oversized bag. She had removed the hats from the boxes they had shipped in. They barely arrived in time. Letti insisted on a cowgirl tea party at the fancy hotel in Denver. The G-mas—a term Letti came up with—were coming on an impromptu trip, something Margaret never did, along with wearing cowboy hats. Fran was good for Margaret.

They planned to meet downtown because Margaret wanted one night in her favorite hotel. But for the rest of the visit, the G-mas would stay with Alex before heading off to Phoenix for the week. Alex was excited and nervous at the same time. Even though her mother had calmed, Alex had many lists she had worked and reworked, making things as close to perfect as she could for Margaret.

Alex and Letti entered the hotel two minutes late. Margaret and Fran weren't in the lobby. Letti's gaze followed the curves of the cast-iron railings that rose above her. "Can we go up?"

Alex nodded. "Oh, yes."

Letti hurried in front of Alex and darted up the stairs in her scoop neck lavender dress with ruffles at the bottom. She wore her pale pink boots and matching hat. Letti was growing so fast. She pranced the around the entire floor, sliding her hand along the metal as she looked down onto the lobby.

After another trip around, Letti sat next to Alex on the red-upholstered chaise longue overlooking the lobby of the grand tea room. "This place is so fancy," Letti said, looking through the railing. "Does Grandmother's house look like this?"

Alex felt an empty spot inside her, like part of painting that had never seen its last stroke. "I'm not sure."

"You've never been there?"

"Nope."

"Why?" Letti looked at Alex with scrunched eyebrows.

"London is far away."

Letti leaned into Alex and asked, "Did you grow up in London?"

"No, you know that. I grew up right here in Colorado."

"Why does Grandmother live in London?"

"She flew back when her mother died. And she stayed."

"I'm glad you and Grandmother talk now. You should go to London someday. And take me. I want to see the inside of her house."

Alex kissed the top of her head.

Letti stood and rested her chin on her hands, which held onto the wooden banister. When Margaret and Fran appeared at the host-stand ten minutes late, Letti jumped and pointed. "There they are."

Alex took a double take. Margaret had chopped her hair. She followed Letti down the stairs. Letti inched herself between the G-mas and took their hands. "You're gonna love your new hats."

Fran knelt down and kissed Letti on both cheeks. "I can't wait."

Letti looked at her grandmother and frowned, informing Margaret, "You lost your hair."

Margaret chuckled and touched the back of her neck. "I didn't lose it, I decided on a new hairstyle. Do you like it?"

Letti put her hand on her hip. "It's okay."

Margaret turned to Alex. "At least she honest." Then she brushed Alex's cheek with her lips and said, "However, I'm not sure about her choice for hats."

Alex tipped her beige hat at her mother, "Yours is black, and you're late, Maggie."

Fran quickly apologized. "My fault. I was on a call and I made your mother wait for me. I'm sorry. I know how she detests tardiness. I will pay for this one." Fran took Margaret's hand.

"Let's not dawdle," Margaret said. "We need to get to our seats."

Letti tugged at the bag Alex carried. "Hats. You need your hats."

Alex set the bag down and Letti pulled them out of the bag and handed them to the G-mas. Once Margaret placed hers on her head, ribbon falling along the back of her neck, Letti said, "Your haircut looks good in the hat."

Letti insisted the hostess take a picture of them. Before any of them sat, Letti had to approve the picture. She sat between the G-mas, beaming. She looked at Margaret. "Are you okay, Grandmother?"

Margaret squirmed in her seat. "Yes, of course."

"You look sad."

Alex noticed her Mother looking at Fran. Her lips tightened ever so slightly and she swallowed.

"Mother?" Alex said.

Margaret answered Letti. "I'm delighted to be in your and your mother's company today. I'm not sad, my darling Scarlett." She took her napkin, placed it on her lap, and kept her focus either toward Letti, the place setting in front of her, or Fran–seeming to avoid any eye contact with Alex.

Alex felt like her soul was trying to push its way out of her body. Something was wrong—really wrong.

When tea ended, the three of them piled into Alex's SUV. Alex handed her phone to Letti, who was sitting in the back seat with Fran. "Can you call Daddy and put him on speaker?"

Letti handed the phone back to Alex. It rang several times before going to voicemail.

"Hey, this is Lukas, leave a message."

"Why can I hear that?" Margaret asked. "Should you be using your cell phone while your operating your vehicle?"

Alex answered, "It's hands-free, Maggie."

"It's not hands-free if you're holding it," Margaret scolded.

Alex held the phone in front of her. "But I can talk without putting it to my ear."

Margaret's tone changed. "You shouldn't be talking on the telephone and driving."

Alex glanced at Margaret. "There's no difference in me talking to you like I am now and me talking on a speakerphone."

She held onto the grab handle above the window on the door of the vehicle, or what Lukas referred to as the chicken handle. "Pay attention to the road."

Alex realized this was all going to Lukas' voicemail. She

left him a quick message. "Baby, we're thirty minutes out. Just wanted to make sure you didn't need anything. And wanted to make sure you picked up dog food today." This was code for him to put the dogs up. She didn't want them jumping on Margaret. Even though her mother had calmed down, Alex was sure the dogs would still irritate her.

"Who are you talking to?" Margaret asked.

Alex held onto the phone. "Lukas. I'm leaving him a message."

"Please, can you use both hands on the steering wheel?" She pushed her hands against the seat and leaned back.

Alex set the phone down without hanging up, frightened of the repercussions that could come with her looking down one more time. She felt like she was fifteen and driving with her learner's permit.

"Why would you call him 'Baby'?" Margaret asked.

Fran interrupted, "For the same reason I call you Lovely."

The car rolled into the garage, Alex put it in park, and then turned off the motor. Only then did she grab her phone and shut it off.

Lukas appeared at the door to Alex's holding his phone. "I tried to call you back, but only got your voicemail."

She leaned in close and kissed him on the cheek. "Don't ask."

After opening the car door for Fran, Lukas removed the luggage from the trunk. "Did you have a pleasant flight, Margaret, Fran?" He's the only one who didn't call her Maggie. The other names he once used for her had evaporated from his vocabulary since she'd, "lightened up." His words.

"We flew in yesterday with the storm. The landing wasn't pleasant," Margaret said.

Fran grabbed Lukas' arm. "I thought she would have to use one of those bags in the seat pocket."

"Are you hungry, ladies?" he asked.

Margaret yawned. "Do you mind if I lie down for a bit? I'm a bit jet lagged."

"That's fine. When you're ready, Lukas will grill burgers if that's okay with you."

"Sounds wonderful," Margaret said.

Margaret's answer confirmed Alex's suspicions. Something was wrong. No matter how much Maggie had changed, she didn't like hamburgers. Ever. Well, she once did, but to Alex's knowledge, her mother had not eaten them since the day Alex's father undercooked them and the beef was bad. Alex remembered the event well. She was ten when it happened. Margaret was so sick. Alex's father still liked to talk about how sick she had been and how she turned green like the witch on Oz. He said the color fit her well. Mean, just mean.

Once Lukas got the luggage, and Margaret and Fran settled into their room, he ran up the stairs. "I took out salmon like you said. Not hamburgers. I thought she hated hamburger?"

"I know."

AFTER THE G-MAS took time to rest, Alex and Lukas put together dinner. The hamburgers weren't mentioned, instead salmon with a buttery lemon sauce, orzo, and asparagus filled their cravings. But there was only small talk made at the table. It was like everyone could see the shadow looming over them, looking down and saying, "Get ready. I'm on my way and there is nothing you can do to stop me."

After dinner, Margaret meandered to the window. “The property is beautiful. Alex, will you take me on a tour?”

Letti sat up. “I’ll show you the donkeys.”

Margaret sat next to Letti. “That would be lovely. But can I walk with your mother alone for a bit?”

Letti sulked. “Okay.”

Fran hugged her. “I’ll help with the dishes and then maybe you and I can play a game. Do you have board games?”

“Do you know how to play Phase 10?”

“One of my favorites.”

Lukas took the rest of the plates off the dinner table. “I’ve got dishes with Letti. You two go for your walk.”

Fran stood. “I’ll help too.”

Alex grabbed her tennis shoes, and her Boston/Poodle mix, Puck, ran to the front door. “Not now, girl.”

They didn’t even get to the end of the drive before Margaret took her hand and squeezed. Alex’s stomach wrenched. It was like she was a fish who had bit the fly on the hook of a fishing pole, right before the person holding the pole at the other end jerked it.

“Mummy?”

Margaret jerked the pole. “I have breast cancer.”

15. THE SIXTH LETTER. EVERYONE NEEDS SOMETHING THAT IS ONLY THEIRS

The urn had its own suitcase for the family trip to California. When arriving at the house they rented in Santa Barbara, Alex opened the hard-shell piece of luggage and found Bessa. Thankfully, the urn wasn't broken. She found a note from TSA informing her they had inspected the bag. Alex removed the tag and handed the pre-printed note to Lukas. "I would have loved to have been a fly on the wall when they opened the bag."

"Right?"

"What the F is this?" Alex said, mimicking them.

"Looks like some kind of vase." Lukas played along, picking up the urn.

"Does it open?"

Lukas pretended to twist the top and look in. "I think it's a body." He looked closer. "That looks like a tooth."

Alex took the urn from Lukas and hugged it tight. "Come on Bessa, time to join the family." She placed the vase on the glass coffee table. "When is Jens coming over?"

"He said he's leaving work around three and we can go to the pier," Lukas answered.

Jens made a compromise for his work to move to Santa Barbara and travel into LA when needed; the position in San Diego didn't open up for him.

Nora and her family would join the group the following day and stay for three days before heading home. Nora wanted to wait a few years to take the kids to Disney, so they'd remember. Alex, Lukas, and Letti would stay for six days, three at the beach with Jens and three in Anaheim so Letti could go to Disney with the G-mas. Maggie and Fran were arriving the following day with Letti. After the fun in California, Alex would fly with Maggie and Fran to Arizona for Margaret's appointments at the Mayo Clinic.

Jens and Lukas shook hands and hugged each other tight. Alex loved that they didn't do the man hug thing.

"Nice house." Jens surveyed the rental.

"I found this place on one of those vacation sites," Alex said. "We're only a few blocks from the beach and now we have a place to gather instead of sitting in restaurants."

Lukas plopped on the couch. "However, we will have to deal with Nora for two days."

"What's wrong with your sister?" Alex asked.

"She's a clean freak."

"You're the clean freak, dude," Jens argued.

Alex argued, "You both are a little OCD. I'd take your sister over both of you."

Jens sat next to his brother and placed his fingertips on the vase sitting on the table. "Mom looks good."

Alex sat next to Jens. "That's an urn."

He grabbed her hand and squeezed and then jabbed Lukas in the side. "How'd you get the good one?"

Alex stood, raced around the table and sat on Lukas' lap. "Smart girls always pick the man."

"Ouch," Jens said.

"Are you going to Disney with us?" Alex asked.

"Hell, no." Jens gritted his teeth.

"See, that's why. A real man would go to Disney with his niece." Alex flicked him on the shoulder.

"She's my little nichy. I love her, but..."

Alex interrupted, "You calling her that, just tells me you were watching *Boy Meets World* in high school."

"Slam," Lukas said.

"I don't have to go to Disney to prove myself to anyone," Jens said.

"Just Letti." Alex argued.

"Where is my girl?" Jens asked.

"She's flying out with my mother. They just spent the week in Arizona."

"How is Margaret?"

"Good, actually. Her hair's thinned out from her treatments. But they got it all. I will spend a few days with her, Fran and Fran's daughter in Arizona next week."

"Nice. Give her my best."

"You'll see her tomorrow."

"Yeah, NOT going to Disney."

EVERYONE EXCEPT MARGARET and Fran gathered in the backyard of paradise. Vines covered the fence that produced flowers the hummingbirds feasted on. The weather was perfect, not too hot and not too cold.

Letti played on the patch of grass with Julia and Eli, who had just awoken from a nap. The adults gathered in plush patio furniture with beverages and a platter of vegetables, meats, and cheeses.

Alex dropped the letters out of the manila envelope that arrived from Wexford, PA.

"Travis' sister lives in Philly, is that close to Wexford?" Nora asked.

Jens lifted his phone and showed a map of Pennsylvania. "Nope. Over four hours away."

Nora held up her phone. "Texted her. She says no."

Jens kept his phone up. "Duh? Map."

Nora flicked him in the head. "Are you five?"

The doodles on the envelope were a book, the Bible to be accurate. Alex turned the purple envelope around. "She must have been feeling religious at this point."

On the back was a quilt doodle with sayings on each block. "You Do You" with a heart, LIVE!, Dream, Be Happy, Be Sad, Be Mad, Do BIG Things, Do small Things, Do ALL the Things In Between, Like, Love, Never Hate. Alex handed the envelope to Nora.

Hello, my wonderfully perfect children. I don't want to talk about who has me anymore.

"Jens is getting you this year, but only because Lukas and Alex brought you with them." Nora leaned into Jens then whispered, "I swear, if you mail her back, I will personally beat your ass."

"Calm down. I promise I will fly back with her. I'll even buy her a seat."

"Don't be a dickhead," Nora said.

Travis opened a beer and sat next to Nora. "This is why I don't sit with you guys through this. Y'all are messed up in the head."

"Shut it." Nora moved away from him.

I'm sure life is happening all around you. Really, you need to figure out what you're going to do with my remains. I recognize I should have planned better. But what I hoped would happen in my life didn't.

I sit here now a little scared of going and I'm unsure. I

should be strong and not go through with this crazy idea, but I don't think any of you are ready to let me go. I'm not ready to go. I should be closer to God. I take that back. I am close to God. I bet you didn't know I read my Bible every day.

Alex paused. Lukas knew. And after she passed, he took the Bible next to her nightstand and took up her ritual. What surprised him was that Bessa had written all over the pages in the book. She had commentary next to several passages. She had written notes which seemed to help her get through different times of her life. She argued with passages she didn't agree with, and in the back she had specific instructions for her funeral.

I took a four-year Bible course with the Catholic Church. They tried to convert me, the instructor, and my classmates. Obviously, they didn't do a very good job. I loved that class. I bet you found my Bible after I passed and wondered, What? Finding all those notes written all over like a true Protestant, but studying with the Catholics. Scandalous! I wanted to do something for myself, and I didn't want to share this time with anyone.

"Don't you have her bible?" Nora asked Lukas.

"I do and I'm keeping it."

"Not trying to take it. But I'd like to see it."

"Only if you promise to give it back."

"I promise."

Lukas stood. "Be right back."

"Is it here?"

Alex answered for him, "He reads a chapter every day."

Lukas returned with the book and handed it to Nora. "You can borrow it for a year, but you have to read it every day. It's what mom did."

Nora took the book, opened to the middle pages, and

shuffled through. She closed it before handing it back to Lukas. "This part of her belongs to you."

He held it in his hand. "I'm willing to share this part with you."

"Always the odd one out," Jens whined.

Nora stood and flicked him on the forehead. "Always the damn baby."

Letti sauntered up to the table and made herself a cracker and cheese sandwich. "You owe me three dollars, Auntie Nora."

"Three?"

"Ass, I think dickhead is a bad word, and damn." Letti took a bite of her food before marching back to the little ones who ran in the grassy area.

Every Thursday for four years I had my night. All mine. It was wonderful.

Do something for yourself. With no one else. Something you love. Share it or don't share it. Do it consistently. Make it meaningful. Keep it safe; don't put it aside to do things for others, because if you do, you will lose yourself and be no good to anyone. Everyone needs something that is only theirs.

Yours for eternity,

Mom/Mama

"Letti," Lukas called. "Do you want me to read your letter to you?"

Letti chased Julia and Eli around. "No. Put the letter next to my bed, I'll read it later." She made a roaring sound, and the babies squealed with joy.

Lukas stood silent.

Alex took the letter. "She's just busy."

16. HE'S NOT A REAL MAN

Nora opened the refrigerator that Alex stocked for their vacation. "The kids are hungry."

Lukas bumped Nora on the side. "Move out." Lukas took meat out of the refrigerator, before turning to Alex. "When is your mom coming back?" After dropping off Letti for the reading of the letters, Margaret and Fran went into town to pick up some things and then back to the airport to pick up Fran's daughter, Beth.

Alex shrugged her shoulders and picked up her phone. She texted her mother: Lukas is putting together a meal. When will you be here?

Maggie: We are almost there. TELL HIM NO COOKING. Fran will prepare the meal this evening.

Alex showed Lukas the text.

"Okay fine." He grabbed a beer from the refrigerator instead.

"I thought we were cooking?" Nora said.

"The mother-in-law says no." Lukas raised his bottle.

"I think we may get a gourmet meal tonight." Alex

squealed. Now that she was close to her mom, she'd had the privilege of Fran's cooking frequently.

Jens checked his watch. "What time are we eating?"

"In a rush?" Nora opened the refrigerator and took out three string cheeses from the drawer and tossed one to Jens.

"I might have a date tonight." Jens tossed it back.

Nora tossed it back. "Give it to Julia."

Eli ran into the room and pointed at his butt.

Nora looked at Travis, who was sitting at the table playing a game on his phone. "It's your turn."

Travis removed a piece of paper from his wallet. "Nope. I had to do the port-a-potty, I still have ten more poop passes."

"Are you counting?" Nora said.

He grinned. "Yep." He grabbed a pen off the counter and put a line on the small piece of scrap paper and then returned it to his wallet.

"You're an ass," she said.

"One dollar," Letti said.

Nora argued with Letti. "An ass is a donkey. You have two. Your uncle is being an ass. Not a bad word."

"You used the word in a bad meaning. Three times now," Letti argued

Nora picked up Eli and headed off to the bathroom. "Nice try."

THE FRONT DOOR swung open and Fran hollered, "You best not have touched that meat."

Alex snickered at Lukas. "Told you."

Lukas took the bags of groceries from Fran. "We'll only be here for three days."

Fran patted him on the arm. "Put them on the counter and thank me later."

Duffel bag and backpack in tow, Beth, Fran's daughter, followed in behind Fran and Margaret. She scanned the room. "Nice place." She dropped the bags by the door. "I love Santa Barbara." When she spotted Alex, she gave her a big hug. "Thank you so much for having me. I didn't want to intrude on your family time."

"No intrusion. You're family. We're glad you're here."

On her way out to the back, Beth passed Jens. Alex caught him glancing up, back down, and then up again. Oh, no, she thought. Alex rushed over to the couch and flicked him in the back of the head. "She's off limits."

He shot off the couch and out the back door, following Beth.

Alex followed him and then changed her mind. She went to recruit her husband to help her. She found Lukas in the kitchen and told him, "Control your brother." She tugged at his arm.

"What?" He pulled away.

"He's out there hitting on Beth."

Fran giggled. "Don't worry, Alex. Beth can hold her own."

"But—" Alex said.

"Don't believe me? Go see her get cheeky with him."

Alex didn't bother to ask what cheeky meant. She headed out to the back and inserted herself into the conversation. She didn't have time or patience to eavesdrop. "Can I get you a drink, Beth?"

"I'd love a glass of wine," Beth said.

"Let me guess, white? Girls like you definitely drink white." Jens asked in a confident tone.

Beth moved closer to Alex. "Did he come with the house

or can we shake him out with the sand that sticks to the rug?"

Alex giggled. "My brother-in-law, but don't worry, he has a date tonight so he won't be staying long."

Beth breathed in the salt air, said. "Red would be good. I'll get it. I'm going to help Paquita with dinner." She strode past Jens, "girls like me, like red." She licked her lips.

"And she cooks," Jens said.

"Niño bonito," Beth used her index finger to tell him to follow.

PASSING BY and finding reasons to go into the kitchen became a game for Alex and Nora. Beth had Jens on a short leash. It was too much fun not to watch.

"Are you crying?" Beth asked him.

"The onion."

"Move over." Beth used her hip to push Jen's out of the way. "Let me do that for you."

Jens dropped the knife. She took the knife and within seconds chopped the onion perfectly. "And that's how you do that without crying like a bebé."

She dumped the peel into the trash and then yanked the bag out of the plastic bin. After tying a knot in the bag, she handed it to him. "Do you know how to take out the trash or do I have to do that for you, too?"

"You're hot when you're bossy," he said.

She pushed the trash into his chest. "Go." Her eyes were bright and her smile was intoxicating.

Alex marched back into the kitchen. "We're all in trouble."

Fran called out. "When you're done with that, you can come mix the dressing."

When dinner was ready, they all sat at the extra-long picnic table in the backyard, eating hamburgers that tasted like gyros on a bun. Margaret even ate one. Jens tried to sit next to Beth, but she placed herself between Fran and Letti.

He took the seat across from her. "At least I can look at you."

"Aw, that's so sweet," Beth nudged Letti. "Your uncle enjoys sitting across from you so he can look at your pretty face."

Letti giggled. "Auntie Nora says he has the hots for you."

Nora cleared her throat. "Sorry. No offense, he has the hots for anything with boobs." Nora gritted her teeth. "That didn't come out right either."

Beth peered down at her chest. "Don't have much there."

Jens scowled at Nora, then took a chug of his beer.

Margaret took over the conversation. "Scarlet, are you excited to go to Disneyland?"

"I'm excited for the roller coasters," Letti said.

Margaret placed her hand on her stomach, "Oh, my."

Jens tried another attempt. "What are you doing tomorrow, Beth?"

She put her arm around Letti. "Going to Disney to ride roller coasters and to meet Mulan. She's my favorite."

Letti giggled. "Uncle Jens won't go to Disney because he's not a real man."

Beth lifted her glass of wine. "Good to know."

17. SOMETHING BIGGER THAN YOU

Letti's voice echoed from Margaret's room. Alex peeked in to see them sitting on the bed. Margaret leaned against a plethora of pillows and Letti leaned against her.

"It's hard to remember her, but I know I miss her," Letti said.

"Do the letters help?"

"Sometimes." Letti paused. "Daddy reads them to me. I've forgotten what her voice sounds like."

Alex hurried back to the kitchen and grabbed the letter. She returned, finding Letti snuggled up closer to Margaret, something she didn't remember doing as a child. Instead of being jealous of the relationship Letti had with Margaret, she was grateful. Because *they* had a close relationship, it rectified the past.

Alex tiptoed into the room and handed Letti her letter from Bessa. "Maybe Grandmother can read to you and it will help you remember?"

Letti sat up. "I'd like that."

Alex left them alone, closing the door halfway before

going to search of Lukas. She found him outside in back alone. "Jens leave?"

"Yep, I think he gave up on Beth."

"Thank God." Alex said. She took Lukas' hand and pulled at him to come inside. "Mother is reading the letter to Letti. I'll tell you why later."

He followed her to the door where they listened. Margaret asked Letti, "Are you positive you want me to read this to you? I don't want to take something away from your parents."

"Yes. I want to hear it from a grandma's voice. I want to remember again."

Dear Letti,

"Do you like Letti or Scarlet better?" Margaret asked.

"Both," Letti said. "I liked the way Bessa would say Letti and I like the way you say Scarlett." Letti rested her head on Margaret's arm.

My sweet most precious girl. What extra things are you doing? Dance? Sports? Choir? Band? 4-H?

"I tried 4-H, I didn't like it very much. I help at the library. They let me come in a few times a week because you used to work there." Letti paused for a moment. "I talk to her when they read me the letter."

Margaret's voice was patient and kind. "That's nice."

"Normally, you have to be a teenager to help at the library. I'm going to join the Teen Advisory Council when I'm twelve. Normally you have to be thirteen."

"That's because you're intelligent," Margaret said.

I hope your mommy and daddy encourage you to do things outside of school. When you were little, you loved to dance. Are you still doing it?

"No. I don't like dance anymore," Letti said.

"What do you like?" Margaret asked.

"I love to read, but you know that. And I love to be outside with the donkeys. I'm going to try basketball at the rec center this year."

"Didn't you play soccer?"

"I didn't like it. Grandpa calls it commi-ball."

Alex looked at Lukas and pounded her palm to her forehead. He whispered. "That's why you shouldn't let Nora take her to see him alone."

Lukas pointed to the room and accidentally tapped on the door.

Margaret look toward the door, then continued talking to Letti. "In London we call soccer 'football'. It's an extremely popular sport."

"That's neat," Letti said.

Whatever you do, find something to be a part of. Something bigger than you. It's okay if you take a while to find something you really enjoy. Changes will happen to you and all the kids around you. Keep busy and have fun. Be the nice kid. The one who listens.

Margaret's voice changed. "I believe you are that person now. I bet your Bessa would be so proud of you." She paused before saying, "As am I."

Alex heard the shuffling of the paper. "Your Bessa would like a favor."

"What?" Letti said.

Spend a day alone with your Daddy, then spend a day alone with your Auntie Nora, and then spend a day alone with your Uncle Jens. The three of them have unique personalities. Together they make the perfect person. If you have cousins, tell them to do this, too.

Love you all to the moon and back.

Forever,

Your Bessa

18. JUST BREAST CANCER

Margaret and Alex strolled through the high-end department store looking for dresses. Margaret wanted nothing too fancy, but she wanted something nice. They planned the ceremony for the end of June. Letti wanted to go to London. She wanted to meet the real Harry Potter. Margaret and Fran wanted the event to be private, only the two of them at the courthouse.

Alex wanted Margaret to be happy.

"I will buy something when I arrive home." They had come back to Colorado after their trip to California and then Arizona. The good news was the cancer was still gone. But Alex didn't want her mom to go back to England.

"Maggie, have you turned into a snob?" Alex asked.

Margaret read the tag on a shirt. "I've always been a snob. Who pays sixty dollars for a polyester blouse?"

"How are you feeling?"

"Fine."

The sales associate moved closer and asked, "Can I help you find something?"

Alex put her arm around Margaret. “She’s getting married at the end of June. We’re browsing.”

“Lovely. Is it a big wedding?” the woman asked.

“Small, very small,” Margaret said.

“Groom doesn’t like big parties?” the woman asked.

“Bride doesn’t,” Margaret said.

“It is your day. You should get what you want.”

“Will he be wearing a tuxedo or a suit?” the woman asked.

“Who?” Margaret asked the woman. It was clear to Alex that the sales associate annoyed her mother. Margaret didn’t like to be bothered while she was shopping.

“Your husband-to-be.”

“Wife-to-be.”

The woman put her hand on her chest. “Is it legal yet?”

“In Britain,” Margaret answered.

“That’s nice. I have a gay cousin—” the woman said.

Margaret stood straight and interrupted, “I’ll let you know if I need help.”

Alex followed Margaret through the racks of dresses. Margaret flipped through them like she was speed reading a boring book. “I don’t want to show cleavage.”

The sales woman appeared again. “If I looked like you, I’d show cleavage.”

Margaret covered her breasts with her hands. “They’re fake. I had breast cancer and chopped the saggy ones off.”

Alex snorted.

The woman didn’t seem to understand Margaret’s annoyance and continued to speak like a tiny little dog that kept yapping at something that wasn’t there. “At least it was just breast cancer. And you got new boobs. I’d do that.”

Margaret halted and spun around. “*Just* breast cancer? You’d do that? You’d get breast cancer to get new boobs?

Have you ever had radiation? Have you ever had your boobs cut out? Not off. Out?" Margaret lifted her hand. "Don't answer. I've had people close to me die of JUST breast cancer. One day I was vacuuming the house, and the next day, they ripped my boobs out. I don't have nipples anymore." Margaret held onto her breasts and said, "I get these. It's like I have an ace bandage wrapped around me all the time. Pressure, always tight pressure. And you want that? Silly little girl, go away."

Margaret told Alex, "I'll get my dress in England." She stomped out of the store. "Just fucking breast cancer."

19. DEBATABLE

It was Eli's birthday, and the family gathered at Nora's. Alex helped Nora with the last of the Hot Diggity Dog Birthday set up. She and Travis had outdone themselves. A huge banner hung from the ceiling above the kids' table decorated with matching plates, cups and napkins. On another table, matching Hot Diggity Bags were filled with party favors in all distinct colors.

The room smelled of onions, chilis, and sugar. Alex supplied the hot dogs from her company. She worked in sales selling a high-end natural sausage. If she ate a hot dog, she needed to know what was in it. The beef in the chili came from T-Bone the Eleventh. Nora didn't like to talk about it, but she loved the grass-fed beef. Eli, Julia, and their friends ran around in the backyard while Letti, Lukas, Travis, and a few brave parents supervised.

The doorbell rang. Nora scanned around the room. "I thought everyone was here. Can you get that for me?" She asked Alex before placing the chalkboard menu on the counter next to the crock pot of chili and stood back to look at it.

Magnus stood alone on the other side of the door, carrying an unwrapped yellow dump truck. “Can I come in?” he asked.

Alex fumbled to open the screen door. “You can.” She held it open, wondering if she should announce his presence or not. She decided not.

Nora peeked around the corner and halted. “Daddy, you came,” she said in a shaken voice.

Alex hiked past the two. She needed to tell Lukas before his father came to the party. When she couldn’t find Lukas, she went back into the kitchen to find wine. She poured a large glass of red, “There will not be enough alcohol to get through this.”

“Get through what?” Lukas snuck up on her.

Alex jumped. “You scared the shit out of me.”

“Mommy, you owe me a dollar. Daddy, Grandpa is here.”

Alex winked at her husband. “Not enough alcohol.” She took a large sip before filling her glass above the approved swirl line, per Wine Etiquette 101.

They followed Letti out to the living room. When Nora spotted the two, she glared at Lukas. Alex leaned in and whispered, “This is obviously important to her. Please try.”

“Hey Dad. What brings you here?”

Magnus staggered over to Eli and scooped him up. “It’s my grandson’s birthday.”

Lukas nodded.

“What’s the nod for?”

“Nothing.”

“I know the nod.”

“Just wondering why Eli? And trying to remember when was the last birthday you showed up for Letti.”

“Son.”

"Okay, so if you don't want to talk about that, why were you still married to mom when she died?" Lukas asked.

"Not here," Magnus replied.

"Why? What's the big secret?"

"It wasn't a secret. She needed health insurance. With the cancer. That's all."

Alex pulled at Lukas. This wasn't the time or the place for this conversation. "Can you help me with the hot dogs?"

"Aren't they done?" Lukas said.

Alex pleaded, "Please. Can you help me?"

When they reached the kitchen, Lukas let loose. "For Eli's birthday? Nice." He examined the contents in the crock pot. "They're done."

Travis trudged into the kitchen. "The sooner we feed everyone, the sooner they leave. I love my kids." He surveyed the room. "But not other people's little ankle biters."

"Let's do this," Lukas said.

Alex monitored Lukas while he helped Travis serve up hot dogs to the kids. Most orders were with ketchup only. Eli insisted on both ketchup and mustard with his dog cut up.

Magnus tried to help. "What can I do?"

Lukas turned his father toward the kids. "Talk to your grandchildren."

Magnus looked over at the folding table filled with kids. "They seem busy and I've outgrown the kids' table."

"Debatable," Lukas said.

Alex walked over to Magnus. "I see your name all over the county. Sales must be good."

"Not bad. I just sold the Polo Ranch to a guy who has no plans of subdividing it. That's a win for us all." He stood tall.

Alex patted him on the back. "A realtor with morals."

Lukas mumbled, "Debatable."

"Lukas," she scolded him.

Magnus took her hand. "It's okay. I deserved that one."

The adults made up their plates and were halfway through their meal when Eli wanted to open presents. Travis stood. "Let's do the cake first."

Magnus' phone chimed, and he glanced down. After reading the text, he stood and went over to Nora. "Sorry sweetheart, I have to go." He paused. "I have... a client that needs me to look into something important."

Nora hugged him. "Thanks for coming."

"Tell me how he likes his present."

"Why don't you give it to him before you go?" Nora said.

Magnus' phone dinged again. "Tell him I love him." He waved around the room. "Gotta go. Love y'all."

ALEX'S PHONE played the song from the television show Once Upon a Time. She answered, "Hello Nora."

"You need to get an Instagram account."

"Are you spying on your stepmother again? I told you she's cray cray and you shouldn't worry about what she says."

"First, that psychotic bitch is not my stepmother. Two, I follow her on Facebook. I'm not sure she has an Instagram. Besides, she's an entirely different story. Three, Jens got an Instagram account and his first post was the urn in its own seat on an airplane. The little dickhead tagged me in it."

Alex snorted. "I wish I could see it."

"Get with the times, Alex."

"Why? So I can stalk people on social media?"

"If you did, you'd know that Daddy and Nancy are fighting."

"I still can't believe he took off right before we sang happy birthday to Eli," Alex said.

"He got a text. I'm sure it was her."

"Now she has this meme about how grandparents matter. I want to tell her, duh shit, bitch. But she isn't my babies' grandparent."

"How are the kids?"

"Perfect. Julia picked more than a dozen of my daffodils and brought them to me today. They are in a vase. It's dorbs. I put it on Instagram. If you had one, you could see."

"You could text the picture to me."

"I could."

Alex could hear the kids on the other side of the phone. "Mama, let us in."

Nora answered them, "No. I'm pooping."

Alex choked. "You're taking a shit while you're on the phone with me?"

"No. I'm hiding. This is the only time they have to leave me alone."

"Mama. Gigi wants in too."

"The dog does not need to come into the bathroom with me."

It was Julia's voice Alex heard next. "Gigi likes poop."

Alex giggled. Their dog had a nasty habit of eating poop.

"Gotta go. Taking the kids to an art class. Love you. Ta ta. See you tomorrow." She ended the call.

A few minutes later Alex's phone chimed.

Nora: Forgot to tell you. I'm going to sell leggings. Will you do a party?

Alex didn't want to.

Alex: Sure. What is Jens' name on Instagram?

Nora: What's yours?

Alex: What is my what?

Nora: You need an account to see his.

"This is a pain." She downloaded the app anyway. She needed Letti's help to complete the task. None of this made any sense to her.

One more text came from Nora. It was the picture of the daffodils.

Letti sat down with Alex. "If you get one, can I get one?"

"Maybe."

"Please," Letti begged.

"Okay."

"What email do you want to use?"

"My personal one."

Letti handed her the phone. "Enter that."

When Alex finished, she handed the phone back to Letti.

"What name do you want me to use?"

"My name is Alex."

"Boring."

"Okay, Mama Alex."

"That's taken."

"What do you mean that's taken?"

"You can't have the same name as someone else. Mama Alex is taken."

"This isn't worth it." Alex said. But then she realized she'd have to have her own account to monitor Letti's.

They set up two accounts with names Letti picked out and Alex approved, and then they found Jens and followed him. She found the picture of the urn strapped into the middle seat of the plane. The caption read, **Taking Mom home. I've had three people change seats. The flight attendant won't talk to me. My sister had better be**

happy; I bought Mom her own seat. He tagged Nora in the post.

Alex texted Jens.

Alex: Your niece is following you on Instagram. Should I tell her not to?

Jens: Nope. Believe it or not, I have put nothing on there I wouldn't want my mom seeing.

She followed Nora and found her page overtaken with legging pictures. And Travis was in all of them. And there were videos. And something about a Facetime live popping up.

"What is Facetime live?" Alex asked Letti.

Letti didn't look up from her phone. "I don't know."

Alex plucked the tablet out of Letti's hands. "You still have a time limit on this."

"Can I get a phone?"

"No."

20. THE SEVENTH LETTER. CRAZY; PATSY AND PRINCE

Even though the sun shined brightly, the temperature didn't rise above fifty degrees. Alex considered moving the gathering to May, but then she'd have to hold on to the letter and not read it. Along with not eating brownies, she had no willpower.

Jens was running late, so Alex poured Nora and herself a second glass of red wine and they discussed who they knew in Italy since that was where the latest letters came from.

"Nobody," Alex said.

"Maybe she had secret boyfriends all over the country and they are sending them to us," Nora said.

Alex leaned on the counter and tilted her head so she was looking up at Nora. "She was still in love with Magnus."

Nora stared at the unopened letter. "Really? What makes you say that? She never talked nice about Daddy."

"But she talked about him all the time."

Nora bit her fingernail. "You're right."

The doorbell rang, and the dogs went nuts. Alex stood. Nora followed her.

They found Jens standing on the other side of the

screen, holding a box filled with purple glass. "I didn't mean to. I really didn't. I dropped it at the airport and—" He shuffled toward the door and then stepped back with his palm pressing his forehead.

Nora fell to the floor and laughed. The dogs ran circles around her and then licked her face.

"You're not mad?" Jens asked.

Nora stood. "It's hysterical. Lukas, however, will probably kick your ass."

"Kick his ass for what?" Lukas appeared behind Jens.

Nora pointed to the box. "He dropped mom at the airport and she's broken."

Lukas peeked inside the box. "No, he didn't." He pushed Jens' shoulder, "That's not the right color purple, and he's missing the ashes. Nice try, dipstick."

Alex made a loud squeal. "You are messed up."

Jens trudged over to the trash barrel sitting on the driveway and tossed the box in it. "It's kinda creepy that you know the exact color of the urn."

"Where's Mom?" Lukas asked.

Jens nodded toward the car. "Strapped in the back seat of the car."

Nora strode out of the house. "I've got her."

Jens scowled at her. "The hot flight attendant wouldn't talk to me because of the urn. Your fault."

"You can thank me later, jackass," she said.

THE KIDS RAN up from the basement when they heard their uncle yell, 'Candy'. Julia and Eli showed their faces first, with Letti following behind at a slower pace.

Jens held out two dum dums for the little ones. Before

they could get them, Nora scooped the candy out of his hand. "After dinner. Maybe."

"Killjoy," Jens said.

He handed Letti a pair of big silver hoop earrings. "If you don't like them, it won't hurt my feelings. I've been told they're cool."

She shook her head. "I love them!" She didn't wait to put them on. She pushed her hair away so everyone could see.

"Super cute," Alex said.

"Daddy look what Uncle Jens got me." She touched the hoops hanging from her ears.

"Super cute," he echoed Alex. Over the past year, Alex had coached him on how to respond to Letti. Alex didn't want them to lose their closeness just because she was hitting her teen years.

Nora touched the hoops. "I want some."

Letti moved her head, and the earring dangled.

Julia's reached up. "I want some too."

"Why don't you go back downstairs and watch your movie," Nora said.

"I want to go see the donkeys," Julia pouted.

Eli repeated. "Donkeys. Donkeys."

"I can take them out," Letti said.

Nora looked to Travis.

"I'll go with them." Travis followed them out.

Once Alex placed Bessa next to the fireplace, she pulled out the letter. "It's from Italy."

"Who is in Italy?" Nora asked.

Lukas sat up and told Alex. "I'm guessing your mother's part of this."

Alex shook her head. "That's crazy. Mother was so jealous of Bessa, and Bessa was aware of that. We talked about it. She didn't understand it, but she was very aware."

"Even more reason. Mom would have wanted to fix that," Lukas said.

"Margaret would never have agreed to that."

"She's come a long way." Lukas said.

Jens held out his hand, and Alex placed the envelope into his. Jens held it up into the light that came from outside. "We could dust it for prints."

Nora grabbed it. "You're a damn idiot."

"You still love me."

"Only because you're my brother." Nora opened the envelope and immediately handed Letti's envelope to Lukas. Then she laughed at the other. On the one side of it the word CRAZY, blocked out, bold, and colored in blue, red, orange, purple and green had been written on it. She took out the letter and handed to Alex, who read.

Who's got me?

Jens raised his hand. "Mom, I had you for the entire year. We hung out in Santa Barbara where you sat next to the window on a table where you could look out at the beach. I had two dates that left the house as soon as they found out I had my dead mom hanging with me. Don't worry, they weren't all that great. One had lop-sided boobs."

Nora slammed a throw pillow into his face. "You are such a damn pig."

"Yep." He pushed the pillow back at her.

Where am I?

"On the fireplace, Mom. You'll be spending this year with Lukas." Jens said.

Do you talk to me?

"Obviously. We're all going crazy," Jens continued to answer his mom's letter.

Lukas said to the urn. "Alex missed you, Mom. She'll like the company during the day."

Before Alex stood, she handed Lukas the letter. She strutted toward the fireplace, picked up the urn, and moved it to the center of the tall table behind the couch. "They can make fun of me all they want. I love our talks. I don't need the urn here to do it. I always talk to you. But I love the touch of purple in my house from time to time, so this is fun." She stuck her tongue out at Lukas and Jens before sitting back down.

Lukas continued to read the letter.

Do you tell people about this? What do other people do with their dead people? This is really messed up. Don't you think? With all of that, I don't believe we are a crazy—Well I take that back; we are a super crazy family, but we're not messed up.

"Oh, Mama. We are more than messed up, we're so screwed up," Nora said.

Lukas scratched his head. "Why do you say that? You guys are good. You and Travis? Right?"

Nora answered quickly. "Oh, we're doing great."

"Your kids are basically perfect," Lukas said.

"Well, Eli likes to run outside with his clothes off. That could be a concern later on. Last week I chased him out the door and he went to the neighbors butt-ass naked and knocked on their door," Nora shared.

"At least it wasn't Travis," Jens said.

"Good point," Nora laughed. "He also sleepwalks. The other night he peed in the corner of the kitchen when we had the neighbors over for a game night."

"Didn't Jens pee in one of his drawers when he was little?" Lukas asked.

Jens nodded. "I also used to pee off the balcony with Dad. Mom would get so pissed. No pun intended."

"Lame," Alex said.

"Why do men pee outside?" Nora asked her brothers.

At the same time Lukas and Jens answered, "Because we can."

"And it saves hundreds of gallons of water when we don't have to flush," Lukas added.

Alex mocked them. "Because we can. Stupid answer." Then told Lukas, "Read."

Do you know what I realized today? The four of us have literally never fought. There is no crazy fighting going on between us. We are lucky. But who knows, maybe we would if my life wasn't going to end. I'd take fights to have more time with you kids.

Lukas said, "We wouldn't have fought, Mom."

It's a gift, weirdly. We will always have the good, and my death will be the only sad. I'm hoping by now you are not sad anymore. Miss me, yes. But don't be sad.

If I haven't got out of purgatory, I'll bet I'm hanging out with all the crazy rock stars who have died and we are jamming out, even though I can't play any instrument. I played the flute in junior high school, but not in high school; I thought I was too cool to do that. It got in the way of my reading. I wish I would have learned to play the guitar. Oh well, maybe they have classes where I'm going.

I'm listening to Crazy by Patsy Cline right now and Jens just came in, he said, "Get over him, he's not worth it."

"I remember that day," Jens said.

I will never get over your father. I wish I had forgiven him.

"Ugh," Lukas passed the letter to Nora to read. "I can't."

Nora continued the pass to Jens. "I'm not reading that shit. Really. Daddy didn't deserve her or her forgiveness."

Jens read.

He tried to come back. Did you know that? It's my only regret; not forgiving him.

Jens stood, dropping the letter on the floor. "Drink anyone?"

The three of them moved to the kitchen, and Alex picked up the letter. Lukas removed the bottle of vodka from the freezer door, Nora found four glasses in the cupboard and put them on the counter. Then glanced at Alex.

"No thanks," Alex said.

Nora placed three small glasses on the island and put the fourth one back. Jens took the cups one by one, filling them with ice, while Lukas grabbed the baggie of cut up lemon from the veggie drawer. Nora poured the alcohol and Lukas added a lemon to two of the glasses. They took their cups, clanged them together and said, "Skol."

Alex finished the letter.

We could have all been together. A little damaged, but not broken. But I never would have trusted him. And you need to have trust in a marriage. If you don't, it can't survive.

But instead of sharing this with Jens, I found that Crazy Prince song and turned it up real loud. Because that was more fun in that moment.

Jens my boy, I want you to know when you read this later, know that as long as you have trust in a relationship, it will all work out. That really goes for all of you. Have trust. And be a little crazy. I love you.

Yours for eternity,

Mom/Mama

Jens scrolled through something on his phone and then set it on the counter for everyone to hear sirens, footsteps, music, then the voice of Prince; "Dearly beloved."

Alex watched the three of them bounce their heads. Nora smiled first, and it was like the scene in *Breakfast Club.* The three of them danced around the kitchen island. It was obvious they didn't notice Alex anymore. They were one, the siblings. Something nobody could break into and nobody should. Alex set the letter down and headed out to see what Travis and the kids were doing.

LATER, Alex stood outside Letti's door and heard her tell Lukas, "I want to read the letter on my own this year."

"Okay," his voice soft and sad.

Alex tapped on the door before walking in. "Honey, can you help me with something?" She paused, looking down at Letti. "I'm sorry, were you guys going to read the letter?"

Lukas hugged Letti. "Letti wants to read on her own this year."

"Can we still read it after you?" Alex asked. "I know it's personal but I enjoy hearing what she has to say to everyone. It gives me a little more of her. I miss her so much."

"Sure. I'll bring it out when I'm done."

"Whenever." Alex leaned down and hugged Letti. "Thank you for sharing her with us."

Alex caught up with Lukas in the hall. "Are you okay?"

"I don't know."

Letti emerged from her room a few minutes later and handed the letter to Alex. "I like it when Grandmother reads to me." She set the letter on the table and trudged back to her room.

Alex snapped pictures of the letter with her phone and sent them to Margaret, before handing it to Lukas. "You read the letter, I'm calling my mother."

Within seconds of hanging up with Margaret, they could hear Letti's voice from her room. Alex pulled Lukas back with her. They stood outside the door and listened for a second.

After Letti responded, "I have a whole summer before I

start. But Uncle Jens bought me the best earrings. I'm going to save them and wear them the first day." Alex and Lukas tiptoed back to the living room. She wondered who Letti was responding to... Bessa or Margaret? It didn't really matter. Love was always love.

"I don't want her to forget my mom." Lukas said.

"I know." Alex sat next to her husband. "Will you read me the letter?"

Dear Letti,

My sweet most precious girl. Ready for Middle school? I'm sure you are, and probably more ready than your parents. I'd like to share things I want you to know about middle school. I know these things because of your Auntie Nora. Girls are mean. Walk away from gossip. Don't get in the middle of it. When they bring you in, look at them straight in the eye and say, "I don't do that." Then walk away. It will be the hardest thing you do the first time. But after that, you will find freedom. And if you get in the middle of it, well, I have pity for you. Ask Auntie Nora how that works and then the next time they suck you in tell them, "Yeah, that didn't work for me so much the first time. I don't do that." Then walk away. Ask Auntie Nora how that works. It is why she is strong, and it is why she had more guy friends than girls. Tell your daddy to get over it, if you have more guy friends than girls. Tell him, I said so.

Forever,

Your Bessa

Lukas folded the letter and handed it to Alex. "I'm not ready for her teenage years."

Alex laughed. "Me either."

21. SPANDEX $$$

Alex invited a few friends and some ladies from the library to the spandex party she was having at the house. When Nora told her to make sure and have enough snacks for forty women, Alex thought she was nuts. She didn't believe that many people would show up. Alex's guest list was twenty. Nora added to it and made sure everyone on social media knew they could bring a friend. Alex had done these types of parties before, and she'd never had a tremendous turnout.

The last count showed forty-five women coming out to her small ranch. Honestly, she didn't understand what the fuss was about. Sure the leggings were soft, but when Nora started hanging them and the other items on the clothing racks, she agreed with Lukas who said, "Who the hell is gonna wear shit with..." he examined the leggings, "are those cheeseburgers on pants?"

Nora pushed him, "Go help Travis bring in the rest of the stuff?"

Lukas did a double-take around the room. "There's more?"

"Yes. Move." Nora pushed him toward the door.

Lukas helped bring in all the boxes and observed Travis helping Nora set it all up.

Travis handed a shirt to Nora. "This should go with the other pink tops."

"Travis, I think you've lost your man card." Lukas walked to the refrigerator, grabbed two beers and said. "Want a beer, or should a get you a glass of chardonnay?"

Travis rubbed his fingers against his thumb. "You haven't seen my bank account. And I'll take a whiskey on the rocks."

Nora nodded at Alex. "You should consider doing this. We've brought in so much money, Travis might quit his job to help me full time."

"Health benefits?" Alex asked.

"We can pay for them and still come out ahead."

"I'll stick to slinging meat. Thanks," Alex said.

Nora kept pushing the issue until the doorbell rang, and the first guest arrived. "You're probably right. Lukas would never do what Travis does."

Travis and Lukas headed into the basement with the kids. On the way down, Travis kissed his wife. "Good luck. If you need help, just say my name."

Lukas didn't look back. "Don't call me."

WOMEN DIDN'T saunter into the house like they did at most multi-level in-home parties, instead they raced in barely even noticing Alex or Nora. They headed straight for the racks. "Can I grab what I want?" a woman who Alex didn't know asked.

"Yep." Nora gleamed. "I brought lots of great leggings. Make sure you fill out a form. There will be a drawing for an exclusive pair of leggings. Also, check the box, ask me how to get free items if you'd like to have a party."

The woman gasped, "I'd love to have a party."

"Who is she?" Alex whispered.

Nora shrugged her shoulders.

Two hours later, six more parties booked, and over two thousand dollars in sales, the last woman left. She was the first one who showed. She ended up being a friend of one of the library ladies. Nora talked her out of purchasing over a thousand dollars of product and instead signing up to sell the clothing line.

As she pulled out of the drive, a black Jeep with red rental plates drove up. Jens hopped out. "I'm back."

Alex pat the hood of the car. "What? You don't call? You just show up, Mr. Random."

Nora ran to him and hugged him tight. "For good, Jackass?"

"For a while, anyway."

Nora grabbed his hand and yanked him toward the house. "Yay!"

He tripped in. "Nora, you need to let me go." Once in, he stopped, taking in the racks of clothes. "What the hell is this?" He picked through a rack.

"I'm selling these." She raced into the bathroom. "Don't touch them."

Lukas and Travis emerged from the basement. Lukas made eye contact with Jens. "Figures you'd be at the legging party. What d'you buy, princess?"

"Go to hell." He grabbed a pair of leggings from a basket and flung it at him.

Travis moved in the middle of them and caught the rolled-up pair of pants. "Boys. This is money you're tossing around."

Jens picked up another pair and tossed them over Travis' head. "Monkey in the middle, anyone?"

"You suck." Travis flung the first pair of pants back at him.

Jens inspected them. "Are these mummy pants?"

"Yep." Travis said holding up the leggings that looked like they were part of a halloween costume.

"Would they fit me?" Jens asked

"Are they tall and curvy?" Travis asked.

"I don't know? What the hell is tall and curvy?"

Lukas grabbed the leggings from Jens. "I'm taking both your man cards."

Jens grabbed them back, dropped his pants, and put them on just in time for Nora to exit the bathroom.

"What the hell are you doing? And what are you wearing under those? You have bumps all over your ass." Nora picked at the leggings.

"Boxers. I can take them off." Jens tugged the leggings down.

"No." Nora covered her face. "You're buying those."

Alex quit laughing long enough to tell them, "This can be one of my free ones."

Jens tugged at Lukas' hand and tried to get him to rub the pants. "You should try these on. They're soft."

Lukas yanked a shirt off a hanger, twisted it, and snapped it at Jens. "Something you wanna tell us? Get the hell away from me."

"Stay away from my dick." Jens covered himself.

"Are you going to take those off?" Nora asked. He looked over at the island in the kitchen. "What's all the food for?"

Alex sighed, "Anyone hungry?"

Jens sauntered over in his new pants and made himself a plate. "Anyone talk to Pops lately?"

Nora huffed. "Nancy blocked me from her Facebook."

Jens took out his phone, brought up Nancy's Facebook account, and handed the phone to Nora. "That's because they got married."

22. THE EIGHTH LETTER. WHAT THE WORLD BELIEVES, AND THE TRUTH

Nora and Travis were killing it with the clothing line. Travis had quit his job and he and Nora were moving into a house three times the size of what they'd had, so Pass the Urn Day was at Alex's. Alex tried to get Jens to have it, but having small children in his downtown apartment wasn't something he found entertaining.

Nora sauntered into the house wearing the trendiest leggings with her kids in tow. "Travis couldn't come, he's shipping today with our crew."

Alex hugged and kissed the kids. "Letti is downstairs and has a surprise for you." Letti had made a mini movie room for the kids and she'd invited Dylan, her 'not-my-boyfriend' boy friend over. They were going to watch Inside Out. Lukas had teased her about using the kids to hang with her boyfriend, which led to Letti ignoring her father most of the day.

"It's outstanding how much your business has grown." Jens grabbed the vodka out of the fridge. "Drink?"

"No, thanks."

"Wine?" Alex asked.

"No, thanks."

"Pregnant?" Lukas asked.

"Yep."

"What?" Alex jumped up and down. "When. How?"

Nora peered at her sideways. "Well, when two people love each other—"

Alex put up her hand. "Stop."

"It happened at the damn conference for work. I was drunk. I forgot to bring my pills."

"Are you happy?" Alex asked.

"Yes, we're happy. We have a lot going on, but we're thrilled. The kids are fighting over what sex the baby will be."

Alex raised her glass of wine. "Healthy."

"Where did the letter come from this year?" Nora asked.

"Austin." Alex said.

"Texas?"

"Minnesota."

"You're jacking with me."

"Nope." Alex handed her the envelope.

Nora examined the stamp. "That's screwed up."

Jens handed Lukas a drink. "Ready?"

"Ready."

They all sat down to read the letter.

My most wonderful, sweet, amazing children.

Reflecting is a weird thing when you're dying.

Jens lifted his glass. "Reflecting is a weird thing when you're alive and not dying."

Nora grabbed her water bottle. "That's because you're an old slut without a family."

Jens directed his glass at her and then Lukas. "I have family."

"I don't mean us. I'm talking wife and kids. Are you ever going to grow the hell up and settle down?"

"If I ever have kids, you'll need to fix that potty-trap of yours."

"You won't have kids."

"Says who?"

"Says me."

I wonder if I've done all the things I should. I've always been a little afraid to die. Where the hell does your soul go?

"If your mom worries about where her soul will go, we're all in trouble." Alex said.

If I go through the cremation thing, will the fire torch my soul? I wonder how many organs they will use? Obviously not my damn pancreas.

Nora started the listing of the recipients of her mom's organs. "Heart, seventy-two-year-old man, who died last year. His daughter sent me a letter to tell me she was grateful for the extra years with her dad. Liver is still working in a fifty-year-old grandmother who sends my kids Christmas cards every year. They sent the gum tissue to the dental school."

Jens held out his hand. "Really?"

Nora smiled. "Really. And, Mama, they're took your pancreas to the cancer center for research." She looked at her brother. "So yes, really."

Jens smiled back. "She was kind of bad ass, wasn't she?"

"Yep."

And, since I have dead people gums, can they can reuse those? I've never wanted to jump out of an airplane, but I wish I had climbed at least one fourteener.

"Letti and I are climbing one this summer." Lukas said.

"Count me in." Jens invited himself.

Lukas told Nora, "We can wait until next year, after the baby is born, if you want to join us."

"Oh, hell no." Nora said.

Lukas asked Alex. "You in?"

"I'm with Nora." Alex winked.

Oh well, I'm not doing it now. Today I would rather spend the day on the deck looking at the most beautiful fourteener from my chair. Enjoy every day like it's the best day, and it will be.

Yours for eternity,

Mom/Mama

Since Margaret was busy for the day, Alex asked Nora to read the letter to Letti. Nora didn't waste any time in calling Letti up.

When Letti reached the stairs, Nora said, "Come on girls, let's go outside on the deck. Get your coats. The view of the peak is perfect." When Nora spoke, people listened. The three of them sat together on the couch Lukas had built into the deck. Nora opened the letter and smiled at her niece. "I get to read you your letter this year. Is that okay?"

Letti shrugged her shoulders. "Sure."

"I'm not one of the grandmas, but Bessa loved you more than anything. She loved you more than she loved me, and I'm okay with that. Do you know why?"

Letti shook her head.

Nora took Letti's hand and said between tears, "Because her love for you would have been her love for my babies." Then she took a deep breath before reading the letter.

Dear Letti,

You are a teenager this year, my sweet most precious girl. How exciting!

Nora argued. "She's lying. Being a teenager sucks. But we're all here for you. We can and will help you get through this. If, and only if, you let us. I had my mom. She helped me through all my screwed-up shit." Nora poked Letti in the side. "No, I'm not giving you two dollars."

The three of them laughed, and then Nora read on.

Oh, how I wish I could be there with you. I got the best of you. You loved me with all your heart. There wasn't a day you didn't want to be with me. Now, I'm sure you are doing all those wonderful teenage things and finding your independence. Hold on to it always. Share the best parts of yourself with the world, toss all the yucky stuff. The world doesn't need any of the ick.

Forever,

Your Bessa

Nora handed the letter to Letti. "Do you remember how wonderful she was to you?"

Letti answered, "Bits and pieces. Mostly feelings. I can't explain it."

Nora sighed. "I wish my kids felt that."

"I'm really trying," Letti said.

"It's okay." Nora brushed the hair out of Letti's face.

"No. You don't understand." Letti looked away. "The movie today. I set all that up because that's what Bessa and I used to do. We would watch movies. She would make popcorn. We would turn all the lights down and snuggle up on the couch. We did that today. Me, Julia and Eli. Dylan came too, but it wasn't about him. You all thought it was about him, but it wasn't. I let him come. But it was all about Bessa."

THE NEXT MORNING, Alex finished packing her bag and then called out to Letti. "You almost ready?"

Nothing.

"Letti?"

Nothing.

Alex walked into her daughter's room, finding Letti leaning against her reading pillow with her tablet in hand. Alex snapped her fingers. "Hello?"

Letti continued to look at the screen.

"Scarlett Jean Larsen."

Letti spat, "What?" The tone, cute when she was four, wasn't so adorable at thirteen.

Alex cocked her head. "What's with the attitude?"

"Why are you yelling at me?"

"Not yelling."

"You kinda are, Mom."

"Trust me. You'd know if I was yelling."

Letti huffed and stared at her tablet.

"Letti?"

Letti answered again, "What?"

"Are you ready?"

"For what?"

"We're leaving for Santa Fe." Alex tapped on her watch. "In five minutes."

"Do I have to go?"

Alex scrutinized her room. Dirty clothes from the week remained draped across her chair and tossed on the floor. "Have you even packed?"

"No."

"No," Alex mocked Letti.

"That's what I said, no."

Alex held out her hand. "Tablet."

"Why?"

"Tablet."

Letti closed the tablet and tossed it on the end of her bed. "Fine," she said, crossing her arms.

Alex grabbed the tablet. "Ya know, you don't have to

come with me. You can stay home with your dad. You have four days to clean up your mess. I love you. See you Tuesday." Alex marched out of the room with the tablet.

"Seriously? I need my tablet for school."

"Use the family computer." Alex didn't look back. She didn't want Letti to see the water covering her pupils. Alex shuffled to the front door where Lukas was waiting.

He held out his arms. "What's wrong?"

Alex took a deep breath. "I'm leaving, she's staying." She put her head into his chest.

Lukas held her. "Are you sure?"

"Nope, but it's best if I go. And now."

"Okay, your bags are in the car. Call me when you get on the road."

Alex nodded her head, kissed her husband, got in the car and drove. She waited an hour before she called him. She took a detour in Colorado Springs at her favorite restaurant and ordered the best spicy Brazilian coconut shrimp soup and ate it in her car—alone. Alex wanted to turn back and get Letti, but the past few months had been rough. Her teen was not that fun to be around. Alex believed she'd get over this phase, but she would not play the game.

Alex called Lukas. "Am I on speaker?"

"Nope," he said.

"You are."

"That's good. Where are you?"

"Just passing the exit for Ft. Carson."

"You want to come back, don't you?"

"I do."

"You need to just go. Enjoy the time with your mom."

"Did you talk to Letti?"

"Yes, and she's still being a putz. So she gets to hang out

with me and her Uncle Jens tonight. We're going to IKEA for dinner."

Alex could hear Letti's voice in the background.

Lukas' voice muted a bit, but his tone was stern. "Yes, you're going."

"But Dad. No fair. I hate that place." Letti whined.

"Yep. Not my problem. Go get ready. We're leaving in two."

"I don't—"

"Now."

Lukas voice softened. "Oh, she's pissed. Have fun with your mom and Fran. Love you."

"Love you."

23. SIT BACK AND WATCH, THIS WILL BE FUN

Alex held the five tickets she'd purchased online for Meow Wolf. She had hoped the immersive experience would be fun for Letti. Beth, Fran's daughter, also suggested it. Beth now lived in Santa Fe and ran a thriving acupuncture and health counseling practice.

Margaret poked her hand. "Do you remember when I caught you sneaking out of the house with that boy?"

Alex chuckled. "Yes. His name was Brett."

"You and I had a terrible fight."

"Yes, we did."

Margaret took Alex's hand. "You and I have conquered many things. You and Letti will be fine. I promise."

Arm in arm, Fran and Beth exited the elevator. Alex nodded in their direction.

"Fran's hand was hurting this morning. She swears the acupuncture works." Margaret shivered. "The last thing that would make me feel better would be to have needles stuck into my body."

Beth leaned in and hugged Alex. "Thank you for letting

me come. I'm sorry about Letti." She tugged at Fran. "Ask my mom, I was the worst teenager."

Fran kissed on Alex before answering. "She was horrible. Boys. Pot. She didn't drink much. I'm just glad she didn't get pregnant. Or marry that boy, whatever his name was. He was the absolute worst."

Beth nodded. "He tried to friend me on social media." She put her finger in her mouth like she was trying to gag herself.

"He's fat and missing teeth, and I'm positive he believes salty snacks are a food group."

A male voice came from behind. "Hey don't take my potatoes away."

Alex turned to find Jens and Letti. Jens grinned and shrugged his shoulders.

Letti ran to Alex. "Sorry, Mommy." Letti couldn't catch her breath. "I wanted— You left— I'm sorry— Daddy—"

Alex held her daughter tight. "Stop," she whispered. "It's okay."

"Are— You— Mad? I—"

Alex smoothed Letti's hair. "Stop. You need to breathe. I'm not mad."

Jens rubbed his hands together. "So, what's this Meow Wolf thing?"

Beth snickered. "You wouldn't like it."

"I might."

"People who don't like Disneyland, probably wouldn't like Meow Wolf."

"I like Disneyland."

"Then why didn't you go with us?"

"I didn't realize it was that important to you."

"It wasn't."

"Then why are you bringing it up?"

Letti giggled, then whispered into Alex's ear. "He talked about her all the way down here."

Alex cocked her head.

Margaret answered the unasked question. "They phoned me to say they were coming. I informed Jens that Beth was here. I also advised him he should go back home after dropping Letti off. Apparently, he doesn't listen."

Jens walked over to Letti. "You riding with me, kid?"

"I want to go with my mom and the G-mas. Is that okay?"

"Great idea." Jens stepped back. He cocked his head to the side and asked Beth, "Wanna ride with me?"

She smirked. "You can ride with me."

"I'm game."

Alex was the first to talk after everyone buckled up. She gazed in the rear-view mirror where Fran sat with Letti. "Fran, I'm sorry."

Fran rubbed Alex's shoulder and leaned forward, laughing. "I don't know what you're sorry about. Beth doesn't know it, but she's got a thing for that boy. And Jens doesn't know it, but she's perfect for him. None of this is for us to worry about. Try to sit back and observe, this will be fun."

24. THE NINTH LETTER. ONE, TWO MORE LETTERS. TWO, MUSIC

When the next letter came, Bessa had addressed it to Alex and Travis. And it was from Ireland. Alex considered Lukas might be correct about her mother being part of this. But she decided not to ask Margaret if she was the one sending the cards. She didn't need to know.

The kids, all but new baby Rowan, were down in the basement. She was taking a nap in the portable crib Alex set up. Letti and Eli watched a movie. Julia stayed in her room playing with the dollhouse Letti had given her. It was a miniature replica of the farmhouse Magnus had lived in when he was a small boy. Magnus and Bessa had built the two-story dollhouse when Letti was a toddler. Outside, the shutters had been hand-painted a deep pink. It was the only thing the home Magnus had grown up in did not actually have. It was hard for Lukas to give away, but easy for Letti. She had told her dad, "Even though I'm forgetting, I still had Bessa. Julia didn't."

Nora came up from checking on the kids. "I forgot Daddy used to sneak over to help Mom build that house. I caught him over at the house a few times when you and Alex weren't home."

Jens sat on the couch looking at his phone. "Maybe they were getting a little nookie on the side?"

Nora flicked the back of his head. "You're sick in the head. Mom had cancer."

Alex put the pot of chili on low and then grabbed the letter. On the outside of the envelope were doodles of two married couples resembling Alex and Lukas, and Nora and Travis. On the other side of the envelope, Bessa had drawn Jens' face. Next to him was a line. Written sideways on the line, she wrote, "Reserved for the love of his life."

Alex handed the envelope to Lukas. "Who's reading? I can't do it since she's writing to me and Travis. I may end up crying."

Lukas plopped the letter on Jens lap. "Earth to Jens. You read."

Jens set his phone down long enough to look at the envelope, smirk, and then fling it to Nora. "You should read. She's writing to your hubby." His phone chimed. He picked it up and viewed something on the screen before setting it down again. His eyes softened.

Nora opened the letter carefully and put the doodled envelope on the counter before sitting on the ottoman in front of the couch.

To my Other Kids, Alex and Travis.

Travis squirmed in his seat. "This is weird. I'd rather hang with the kids during this and read it later. Can we just stick to that tradition?"

Alex grabbed his arm. "No."

I have never overlooked you two. I love you as much as I love my own children.

Alex,

Alex could feel Travis relax. "At least you're first," he said.

A friend once told me, "You only get your sons for a little while, cherish the time you have with them because when they marry, you'll lose them." She was wrong. I never lost Lukas. You have been the best daughter-in-law.

Nora leaned in and grabbed Alex's wine from her and took a sip. "Nursing sucks. But I'm allowed a few sips." She handed Alex back her wine and then said, "You really are the best. You could have been a holy terror like Jens' girlfriends."

"Hey," Jens said. His focus remained more on his phone than the conversation.

Nora leaned toward him. "What's so intriguing on that phone?"

Jens shoved it in his back pocket. "Nunya."

"Nunya?"

"Nunya business."

"Some floozie, I'm sure."

"Isn't mom trying to talk to Alex? Being kinda rude, don'cha think, Sis?"

Nora flipped him off and then continued.

You wanted to travel the world. Instead, you moved onto ten acres with your husband and daughter to take care of his dying mom. I bet you're still on that ranch taking care of those donkeys and cattle. You don't have to stay.

Alex put her hand on her chest. "But I don't want to leave."

Lukas will follow you wherever you go.

Lukas took her hand and whispered. "I would."

Alex took in her world. "I don't want to."

I made him promise me he would. Although, he laughed at me when I did this. He said, "Mom, there isn't anything I

wouldn't do for my wife. I will spend the rest of my life making her happy, whatever she wants is hers."

Lukas nodded. "I said that."

Now would be the time to ask for anything. Like dishes for life. Laundry for life. Foot rubs every night—FOR LIFE!

Alex put her index finger to her mouth. "Hmm."

Lukas laughed. "Don't even try."

Nora put the letter down. "Oh, I'd try. Do you need paper and pen? I'll help you with the list."

Lukas tapped Nora with his foot. "Read the letter, brat."

I just want to thank you for being my daughter. Neither you nor Travis are my In-Laws. I'm forever grateful for you.

One favor? Please don't let Jens marry some high maintenance girl. I've already asked Nora to make sure he doesn't. He may need the both of you to make sure this does not happen.

Jens huffed, "Wow, Mom."

Love you, girl!

Bessa

Nora grinned at her husband before she started reading.

Travis,

Even though you and Nora are not married as I write this, it doesn't matter. I believe with all my heart that you will always be together.

Nora looked over the paper at Travis. "He married me Mama."

Travis winked. "No commentary. Just read. I don't like this."

Nora rolled her eyes. "Okay."

I gained a son when you moved back to Colorado. I don't think you wanted to leave the Carolinas. You love the water and you had the best job.

Jens blurted out. "He sells spandex now, Mom. And I've seen him put on the clothes on video. I'm concerned."

Alex kicked Jens. "This from the boy who lets his nieces paint his toenails."

Travis shuffled again. "Look, I'm good in my skin. He can paint his toenails and I can model on video. Can you finish the letter?"

You sacrificed so Nora could be with me. You will never understand how much this has meant to me. You gave me the gift of my daughter. She and I have had so much fun the past few years. Even now, as my body continues to give out, she and I have time. Time is precious. You are a great husband, a wonderful son, and if you choose, you will be the greatest Daddy.

You and Lukas can get in on the Jens thing too. I believe you and Lukas married some wonderful women.

Love you, Travis.

Bessa

Travis leaped up. "I'm going down to check on the kids."

Nora handed the letter to Alex. "Will you finish?"

"Yep."

To my wonderful, most AMAZING children,

I want to prepare you all. There are only two more letters.

Alex's heart stopped beating. She observed the panic in the siblings' faces appear. She swallowed.

Next year you will get two. One on the anniversary of my funeral and then another one a month later. You need to do something with this urn.

I love you all.

Yours for eternity,

Mom/Mama

The room was silent.

. . .

ALEX AND LUKAS laid in bed. Alex reading a book and Lukas fiddling with the Letti's letter. Alex laid her book down. "Are you going to read the letter?"

"She's going to stop writing."

"Yes."

"I don't know if I'm ready."

Alex wanted to say she wasn't ready either.

Lukas held the letter up. Letti wouldn't let anyone read her the letter this year. She said she didn't remember anymore. She said she didn't feel close anymore. But after she read it, she smiled and told her parents, "Even if I don't remember Bessa, I know she loved me."

He didn't read it out loud. It took him a bit to get through it. He had to set it down a few times to blow his nose. When he finished, he handed the letter to Alex.

Dear Letti,

My sweet most precious girl. Two things.

One, thank you for taking care of my girls. But if your parents want to go travel the world, let them. I'm sure they won't leave until you graduate, but if you all want to go, find a good home for the girls and go! It's okay.

Two, Music. I want to share my favorites. I believe music is one of the best things in the world. Listen to it! All of it. All kinds, especially the stuff that makes you happy! Go to concerts. The last concert I attended was John Mellencamp, you all came with me and we had excellent seats. Do you remember? I remember we all laughed, and we all danced. One of the best days ever! The best concert I ever saw was the Beatles at Red Rocks. If I had to think of some of my favorite songs, it would be:

'Burning Love', by Elvis Presley

'Crazy', by Patsy Cline

'Respect', by Aretha Franklin

'(Sittin' On) The Dock of the Bay', by Otis Redding. This was the first song your grandpa and I danced to. We met in 1969. This was the best day of my life.

'Sugar, Sugar', by The Archies.

'Here Comes the Sun', by the Beatles. I believe this is my ALL-TIME FAVORITE SONG! The sun always comes out. There is a quote by Rose Kennedy. Find it; it's about birds and storms.

'Joy to the World', by Three Dog Night. Jeremiah was a bullfrog. Sing it!

'Crocodile Rock', by Elton John. This was the year your daddy was born. This was the song all the kids and I would dance to when they were growing up. You and I danced to it too!

'Kodachrome', by Paul Simon. Pictures. Take tons of them!

'Landslide', by Fleetwood Mac. This was the year your Aunt Nora was born.

'Mr. Blue Sky', by Electric Light Orchestra. Because you love this song. Remember how we used to play this song while you swung on the playset in the backyard?

'Silly Love Songs', by Wings. This was the year Jens was born.

'Heart of Glass', by Blondie

'Sweetest Thing', by U2

'Love Shack', by The B-52s. You know my rule. When this song comes on, everyone must sing at the top of their lungs when appropriate and dance!

'Right Now', by Van Halen

'Gettin' Jiggy wit It', by Will Smith

'Love Story', by Taylor Swift

'So What', by Pink. Because at 65 I'm still a rock star, even if I'm dying. And mean people are Tools. Don't forget that, Letti! Mean People are TOOLS! Be a nice person. Be a kind person. At least try.

Music tells a lot about a person. I bet if I started this list tomorrow, my picks would be different.

What is your favorite music? Ask the old people what their favorite music is.

I decided early I would not let my age define the music I listened to. However, life sometimes dictated what I listened to. I turned up what I loved and sang as loud as I could. I have a magnificent voice in the shower and in my car, as long as I roll the windows up.

One last thing. Everything always works out and we always make it—even when we don't. My death is a passing in time. I've lived and loved beyond anything I ever could have imagined. I hope you do the same!

Forever,

Your Bessa

"God, I loved her," Alex said.

"Me too," Lukas' words were barely audible.

25. IS HE GOING TO DIE?

After making ten calls to meat managers who didn't have time to talk to her, Alex pushed her phone to the side and took a walk. Before heading out, she put her dog, Puck, on the leash. Bishop, her husband's new foster-fail sat behind the gate and whined. He wanted to go, too. "If you weren't such an ass, pulling and yanking me, I'd take you, too."

A storm was coming, but at that moment the temperature was sixty-five degrees and the sun made it feel warmer. Alex hiked with her dog along the two-mile dirt road loop without a single car passing them. The dog wandered from side to side, sniffing all the things. The alpacas behind a fence hummed as they passed. Puck halted.

"Leave it," Alex said. "I know you just want to make friends with them, but they are bigger than you."

The white geese in the next pasture honked loudly. Alex remembered one of her first times coming out to the ranch. She couldn't figure out what animal was making the sound. The noise wasn't the typical honk of the Canada Geese that flew overhead. To Alex, they sounded like they were crying.

The last quarter of a mile was extra quiet, Alex took a deep breath in. "The calm before the storm, Puck. We forget to breathe."

When they arrived back at the house, Bishop sat at the door, ears erect, waiting for his turn. "You'll have to wait for Daddy," Alex told him as she took off Puck's leash and hung it in the laundry room.

Her phone chimed several times in a row. She picked up the phone to see several missed calls and text messages. She read the messages first:

Lukas: Call me

Lukas: ASAP

Lukas: It's my dad.

Lukas: At Adventist. Please come as soon as you get this.

Lukas: I haven't told Letti.

Jens: He's not dead

Jens: The hag is here...

Jens: She's so bitter

Jens: She's hideous

Nora: I'm here at the hospital. Lukas is okay, but if you could call that would be good. He has NOT told Letti.

Lukas: I do not deserve you. I'm an ass. Why did you marry me?

Lukas: You should have married my brother. He's buff, the chicks dig him.

Lukas: My brother is an ass! Jens took my phone.

Alex was grateful for the joke. Only because that meant there was at least a pause for Lukas. But then again, it also meant she was out on her walk for too long and not there for him. She felt guilty, but she hadn't known. She needed to get to Lukas.

Lukas: I'm not sure how long Dad's been in surgery.

Nancy told them not to tell us anything. I want to punch the bitch in the throat!

Jens: Your husband has no sense of humor. But seriously, where are you? He really needs you right now.

Alex responded to Lukas: Sorry, was taking a walk. On my way! I will pick up Letti.

When he didn't respond she sent a quick text to Nora: On my way.

Then Alex dialed Lukas, who picked up on the second ring. "Hi, Baby."

"I'm so sorry. I was on a walk with Puck. I didn't bring my phone. How is he?"

His voice cracked, "They won't tell us anything. And that bitch won't either. I'm gonna—"

Alex interrupted, "Don't do anything. I'm on my way. I will pick up Letti. Honey?" she paused, "I love you."

"Love you too."

ALEX AND LETTI exited the school. Alex walked, Letti stomped. When Letti was three-years-old, she begged Alex to take her to school. She wasn't satisfied with the couple of hours at the local preschool run by the Methodist Church. She wanted to take the big yellow bus and go every day, all day.

"Why do I have to leave early?" She stood on the concrete between the front doors of the school and the parking lot.

"Sweetie, Grandpa Magnus is sick."

She rolled her eyes. "Is he going to die?"

Alex rubbed her forehead. "I'm not sure."

Letti slung her pack over her shoulder and headed for

the car. "We better go before he needs his own glass container. Uncle Jens won't let him share with Bessa."

Alex stood grounded in front of the school. "Letti. That is horrible. He is your grandfather."

"Nobody even talks to him. He barely talks to us. How do you expect me to feel?"

"Fair enough," was all Alex could say.

FOLLOWING FIVE OTHER PEOPLE, Alex and Letti stepped into the elevator. Alex punched the button to the third floor several times upon entering, hoping it would make the trip faster. The door shut, taking all the air. "Too crowded," Alex mumbled to herself.

"Two, please," a woman's voice said.

"Four," a man said in a demanding voice.

Alex pressed the button. *Rude.*

"Will he'll be dead when we get there?" Letti whispered in Alex's ear.

"What floor for surgeries?" a man in a suit asked.

"No, I doubt he's dead. He's too ornery."

The man spoke at Alex without looking at her. "I'm trying to find surgeries, I said nothing about someone dying."

Alex pointed to Letti, "Oh, I'm sorry. I was talking to my daughter. She's worried about her grandpa. I believe it's the third floor."

The door opened on the second floor, and two people exited.

Alex again pressed the button for the third floor several times and the door shut.

The man in the suit huffed. The elevator moved up

another floor, and the door opened. He shoved past Alex and exited.

Alex and Letti followed the man out the door and toward an information desk where a woman sat. The man demanded, “Surgeries, is this where surgeries are? I’m looking for my wife.”

Alex saw her clan to the left and nudged Letti. When Lukas noticed them, he stood. Alex rushed over and held him tight. She knew this was hard for him. He once idolized his father. Thought the man did no wrong until Magnus did the worst. And the worst wasn’t even cheating on his wife, Bessa. The final straw was when Magnus walked away from his own children.

When Lukas relaxed a bit, Alex asked, “How is he?”

“According to the hag, he doesn’t want to see us.”

“It will be okay.” Alex softly rubbed Lukas’ back. She then stepped closer to Nora and Jens and sat between them, taking their hands into hers. “Can I get you anything?”

“Someone to tell us what is going on?” Nora said. Her words were scratchy and broken.

“Travis with the kids?”

“Yes.” Nora stood and said, “I should call him.” She stumbled out of the room.

Alex patted Jens’ hand. “You okay?”

“I’m fine. I’m only here for Lukas and Nora. I’m supposed to leave tomorrow. But now I have to stay… because I promised Mom.”

“You promised your mom what?”

“Before she died, she made me promise if anything happened to *him*. I’d always be here, no matter what jacked up things he ended up doing.”

Alex couldn’t help let a small snort escape. “I bet those where her exact words too.”

His face lit up. "Exact."

She patted his hand again. "You're a wonderful son."

A shrill, whiny voice that cut into Alex's core moved toward them. Nancy appeared, "Which one of you told them I'm not his wife?" Her face puffed and red, black circles under her eyes made her look like the monster Alex believed her to be. Nancy's breath heaved, like she just finished climbing the Manitou Incline.

Alex cringed. She looked at Lukas.

He shook his head.

She then tiled her heat at Nora who mouthed, "I wish."

Then Alex looked at Jens. "I've been sitting here the whole time. Besides, I thought they got married. Wasn't that the last social media scandal?"

Nancy continued her tirade. "We've been together for over ten years."

Jens chuckled. "Not consistently."

"You're so smart aren't you, Jenny Boy."

Jens clenched his fists.

Lukas chimed in. "Has he married you yet?"

"That's none of your business," she huffed.

Letti strode into the room. "He won't marry her. He promised Bessa he wouldn't."

Nancy took Kleenex out of her pocket and dabbed at her eyes.

"Seems to me, legally, we're family, you're not," Lukas said.

"If we split up, we'd still need a divorce," Nancy wheezed.

"I keep praying." Lukas put his hands together and then did the sign of the cross.

A doctor appeared wearing blue scrubs, still in his cap.

He addressed the room. “He’s out of surgery. He did well. Now he needs rest.”

Lukas stood with his hand held out. “I’m Lukas, Magnus’ son.”

The doctor frowned. “I didn’t know he had a son.”

Jens jolted out of his seat, standing erect. “Two sons.”

Nora followed her brothers and said, “And a daughter.”

Nancy pressed her hands against her pants, smoothing the wrinkles out, strutted toward the doctor and said, “Can you show me to his room?”

“Nancy, I’m sure he’ll want to see all of you soon, but right now he’s still in recovery. They should move him to his room within the hour.”

“But I’m his-” she abruptly stopped talking, and shuffled away.

The doctor pulled off his cap and said, “I’ll have the nurse’s station keep you updated. I don’t have a card on me, but I’ll give you my number and you can call me if you need to. Once I’m able to talk to your dad, I’ll either be able to share or not share more of his diagnosis with you.”

26. BESSA, ARE YOU WATCHING THIS?

Alex picked up the closest magazine and browsed through the pages. "Does anyone even read magazines anymore?" The silence answered her question. Lukas, Jens, and Nora had their noses stuck in their phones. She read aloud from the pages. "When your toddler embarrasses you in public."

Nora giggled. "I have a story. Last week, we were out having dinner and Travis took Julia to the bathroom. The family bathroom was occupied, so he took her into the men's room. After she was done, he went. As he was peeing, she moved to see what he was doing. She nodded her head and said loudly, 'So that's how YOU do it.' Apparently, there was a burst of laughter from the other occupants. Now every time Travis goes to the bathroom, she thinks it's funny."

After Alex was done snorting, she said, "Did I ever tell you the story about Letti taking a shower with your mom?"

"Oh, God. Please don't Alex," Lukas pleaded.

"Do tell." Jens put down his phone.

Nora twisted her face. "I'm a little frightened."

Lukas dropped his head into his palm, "You'll wish you hadn't asked."

Alex giggled. "When Letti was three or four, she'd take showers with me. When we moved into the house with Bessa, she asked if she could take a shower with her one night."

Lukas stood and tromped out of the room. Jens moved in front of him to block him from leaving.

Alex continued. "When they finished, Letti came upstairs and said, Bessa has a BIG Lellow flower. She needs to cut it like Mommy's."

Jens grabbed hold of Lukas' shoulder, spun him around, and they raced out of the waiting room. Nora couldn't stop laughing.

Alex shook her head. "Boys. They forget their mama ever had a vagina."

Letti shuffled in. "What's so funny?"

Nora snorted, "Bessa's Lellow Flower."

Letti rolled her eyes. "Are you torturing Dad again?"

"And your Uncle."

"That story isn't funny anymore," Letti said.

A woman appeared to gather the family to see Magnus. Nora pulled at Alex. "Come on. He's always liked you best."

Alex argued. "Not true. I'm the only one who doesn't pick on him, so he uses me to get out of trouble with you guys."

Lukas and Nora stood next to their father's bed, Jens waited at the door, and Alex found a spot in the corner of the room. When Magnus opened saw them, he searched out Alex. She moved to Lukas' side. Magnus followed her with his eyes. "Do you think they'll ever forgive me?"

Alex tugged at the end of her hair. "They're right here. Ask them, not me." She scoped the room, found a chair in a corner where he couldn't see her, and sat. She mouthed into the air as if Bessa was there, "This is not my circus, but you sure left it to me, didn't you?"

"They say you'll be fine, Daddy." Nora's pressed her palm to her heart.

Magnus opened his hand, and Nora allowed hers to drop into it. Then she kissed her father's forehead and whispered something Alex couldn't hear.

"I missed you, too." He nodded to Lukas. "I see the gray found its way to your unshaven face. Girls do that to you."

"And fathers," Lukas added.

"Jenny? Are you gonna talk to your old man?" Magnus asked without looking at his youngest son.

Jens looked past his father and out the window. "Still thinkin' about it."

There was a tap on the door that was slightly ajar, and her voice crept in. "Magnus?"

Jens used his foot to push the door closed. "If she comes in here, I'm out."

"I have to talk to her," Magnus said.

Jens opened the door, gave Nancy the death stare and said, "He's all yours."

Alex stood.

Magnus raised his hand. "Let him go."

Nora backed away from her father. "You can't keep letting us go, Daddy."

"He's the one who left." Nancy huffed.

"Enough, Nancy. This is between me and my children."

"But I'm your–"

"Not his wife," Lukas finished.

Magnus closed his eyes. "Maybe it would have been better if the heart attack took me."

"See what you did?" Nancy said.

"What I did? You are the—"

"I'm what? You shouldn't talk to your father that way. My kids would never talk to him that way."

"Nope. Your daughter is out there taking her clothes off and shoving coke up her nose while my father pays attention to her kids instead of mine."

"We love our Letti. She knows Granny and Papa love her."

"You are not my daughter's Granny and she doesn't call him Papa, she calls him Grandpa."

"God forbid anyone takes The Great Julia's place. She wasn't perfect." Nancy crossed her arms.

Alex stood. "Stop," she said firmly in a calm voice. "Just. Stop."

A nurse opened the door and said in a stern voice, "I think Magnus needs some quiet time. Along with the rest of the patients on the floor."

Nancy put her hands on her hips. "They can go. I'm staying with my—"

Magnus cleared his throat and said, "Actually, I'd like everyone to go except Alex."

Nancy quivered her head like she was having a mini seizure, crossed her arms, huffed, then spun on a heel, and stomped out the door.

Lukas kissed Alex's cheek, "That's what you get for being the balanced one."

Alex hugged him. "You so owe me."

"I know."

ALEX SLID the chair to the side of the bed and sat. Magnus smiled. She smiled back. "Well?" he said.

"Well?" she said back.

"You're going to make this hard, aren't you?" he asked.

"I'm not making anything hard."

"Are you saying I am?"

"I didn't say that."

They sat. He gazed at her and then out the window. He closed his eyes, and she closed hers. Alex counted in her head. "One, do not start this conversation. Two, he's baiting you. Three, Bessa, are you watching this? He's driving me crazy. Four, Bessa, this is where Lukas gets this from—the silence—but Lukas has the good side of you even if it amounts to exploding. Five, I wish I had brought you today, yes the urn, remind me to bring you next time. Don't laugh at me, I'm serious."

"What are you smiling about?" Magnus asked.

Alex opened her eyes. Magnus picked up the remote and examined it. He pressed a button that moved the bottom of the bed where his feet were, lower. "How do you work this thing?"

Alex held out her hand. "What do you want it to do?"

Instead of handing her the remote, he grabbed another remote and pressed buttons on both devices. The lower part of the bed moved up, the television popped on then off, the entire bed lowered, the television turned back on then off again, then a voice echoed through the room, "Did you need something?"

Alex stood, grabbed the remotes and said, "Sorry, he's good. Thank you." She raised an eyebrow. "What are you trying to accomplish?"

"I want to sit up." His tone reminded Alex of Letti when she was little and frustrated.

Alex stood next to him with the remote for the bed. She pointed to the top of the rectangular white device. "The arrows on the side of where it reads Head, make the top of the bed go up and down, see?" She pressed them so he understood. "Foot." She pointed to the remote, pressed the button. "Up and down. Same with the bed." She pointed to the word Bed. "The red button is to call the nurse's station. Don't bother them unless you need something, they're busy." She paused and then gave him the look she gave Letti when she was scolding her. "I mean it." She showed him the other remote. "This is for the television. On and off button." She pointed at the red button and then other buttons, "channel, volume." She placed both gadgets next to him and sat back down in the chair.

He adjusted his bed and swallowed. "I still miss her."

"So do I." Alex said.

"Do you think the kids will ever forgive me?"

"That's up to you."

"But they won't even talk to me."

"You don't return their calls."

His gaze darted away from Alex.

"Listen Magnus, I love you. I can't fix your relationship with your kids. Either you want one or you don't. They've tried to call you, they've tried to text you, and they've even tried to reach out to you on social media. Either you're ignoring them or Nancy is deciding for you. Either way, it's messed up. People don't walk out on their kids."

"They don't need me anymore."

"I call bullshit." Alex squeezed his hand and stood.

"Please don't go. I don't want to be alone."

"Call one of your kids and you won't be." Alex didn't look back because she knew she'd end up staying.

27. WHAT'S WRONG WITH YOU PEOPLE?

"Alex, have you seen mom?" Lukas' voice floated out of his study and up the basement stairs.

"Here we go." Alex rubbed her hands together. She loved Pass the Urn Day. It was bittersweet knowing it would end soon. She bobbed her tea bag up and down in the oversized pottery cup Lukas bought her at the local farmer's market. Apparently, perfect tea should be brewed between three and five minutes. She wasn't counting. The aroma of the licorice and orange peel filled the surrounding space. "More is better today," she said to herself.

"Alex?" Lukas called out again.

She let go of the string and stole a sip of the tea before tiptoeing down the hall, passing the front door and the plant she had to move out of their bedroom because its green leaves touched the ceiling. The plant, a gift from Nora when Letti was born, reminded her how fast time moves. She tapped lightly on Letti's door. Letti's honey chestnut hair stuck up out of the blanket. Wrapped in her comforter like a burrito, Letti didn't move. Horns in the spot between her eyes appeared. Those horns only materialized when Letti was irritated or mad. Lukas said she looked part Romulan when she did this. Alex didn't agree. She loved the horns. To Alex, her sweet daughter's horns were a beautiful rotten sweetness only a mama could understand.

Alex took quick small steps to the other side of the bed, dodging the chaos scattered across the floor, until her big toe slammed into the wicker basket hiding at the corner of Letti's bed. "Shit," Alex whispered before crawling in beside Letti and pulling the sheets over her own head.

"Mom." Letti tugged at the covers. "Are you seriously hiding from Dad?"

"Shh," Alex answered.

Letti rolled herself loose, kicked the covers off both of them, and hollered, "Dad, she's in here."

Alex reached for the sheet but couldn't quite reach it. She pinched Letti on the side. "Brat."

Two quick knocks on the door and a pause.

"Come in." Letti sat up. "Let's get this over with."

Lukas asked, "Do you know where your Bessa is?"

Letti pulled the comforter up around her. "No," she huffed. "I know where she should be though. Buried in the ground. Or, maybe under a tree, or spread those ashes somewhere, anywhere, instead of passing her around from family to family in that obnoxious container."

"Remember, you helped pick it out." Alex reminded her.

"What does Auntie Nora do with her for the year? Or Uncle Jens?" Letti slid down into the bed, rolled on her stomach and covered her head with the pillow.

After kicking the sheets off her feet, Alex examined her toe. A tiny sliver of the basket made a home in her skin. "Got tweezers?" Alex yanked the pillow off Letti's face.

"In the bathroom."

Alex asked Lukas, "Will you grab them?" Alex messed with Letti's hair. "Your room is a disaster. An aftermath of a tornado is tidier than this."

Letti rolled her eyes. "Quit being so dramatic."

Lukas appeared with tweezers. Alex stuck her foot in the air. "Save me. Save me."

"Oh, my gawd, Mom."

After Lukas removed the splinter, Alex rolled off the bed, making sure she missed the basket before standing next to Lukas. "Jens' girlfriend won't allow the urn in the house." She kissed her husband on the cheek and then winked at Letti. "She's in the corner of your closet, Letti," she said before exiting the room.

"Mom. I can't believe you."

Alex peeked back through the doorway. "If you cleaned your room, Letti-girl, you'd know she's been there for the past two months."

"What's wrong with you people?" Letti stomped over to her closet, shoving it open. Behind a pile of notebooks, an old blanket, and a sweatshirt, sat the speckled glass vase. Letti grabbed the sweatshirt. "I've been looking all over for this." She chuckled, stepped to the side and pointed to the urn and said, "Daddy, you get her. I don't want to break it." Her horns disappeared, and she puckered her lips together and made a smacking noise. "I wonder what our priest would think about this passing of the urn? Maybe I should ask him."

"You wouldn't dare, Scarlett Jean." Lukas said.

Letti raised her left eyebrow before turning away and strutting out. She mumbled under her breath, "I just might. I think the Catholic Church expects a person's remains to be buried, not sure why, but I think they do."

"I can't hear you when you talk and walk away," Lukas

said, following her.

Alex trailed behind them. Letti poked at her dad and giggled, "Don't drop her."

WHILE LUKAS and Letti attended mass, Alex sat at the high wooden table in the area between the kitchen and the living room. She'd replaced the ficus bonsai centerpiece with the urn. Alex sipped on her second cup of tea, this time an apple green tea with too much honey. She cleared her throat and then placed her hand on the glass container. Unlike Bessa, it was hard and cold, but like her it was beautiful. "I still liked the speckled hot pink one better," she said.

Then she continued the conversation as if Bessa was there in the room defending her choice. "Whatever, the metal would last longer and there wouldn't be a chance of it breaking."

"Be aware, you're not allowed to break in my house. As much as I love you, I don't want to be finding particles of you for the rest of my life."

She took another sip of tea before standing. Alex pressed her forehead against the west windows where the bee hives nestled against the double rows of lilacs. The entrance to the boxes faced the morning sun, and Alex could see the activity around the entrance of the hive. Alex spoke to the bees, "Sorry, kids," while pouring the tea into the sink. She hated wasting the honey they work so hard to make.

Alex leaned against the heavy granite composite farmhouse sink Lukas installed with the remodel of the kitchen and continued to talk to the urn. "Remember the first time I came out here? Lukas took me for a stroll around the property and to show me where the honey came from. I'm not sure what I thought would happen. Honey magically appearing in glass jars or plastic bears? When we got close to the hives, I heard the buzzing close to my ear and ran screaming back toward the house. Instead of laughing at me, you smacked Lukas, telling him he should have warned me."

"I know. I know. I still married him, and I'd do it over again and again. He was so handsome. Still is," Alex gazed out the window again. "The crocuses are popping. If the deer don't get them, it looks like we'll have all three colors this year. Letti's favorite is still purple. Mine is yellow."

Bishop leaped off the couch and tore out the dog door, followed by the piercing bark of Puck. The tires of Lukas' jeep hit the drive.

Alex sat at the table. "I planted tulips in the planters out front last fall, I'm hoping they made it through the winter. It was colder this year. And they say snow is coming."

The front door opened, and Lukas flipped off his shoes in the entryway. "Are you talking to the urn?"

Alex shrugged her shoulders. "After all these years, you're still surprised?"

Letti planted herself in the tall chair to Alex's right, then educated her on Catholic rules. "The deacon says we should *not* keep the remains of a dead person in the house. Catholic teaching says the dead should have a proper mass and burial."

"Good thing your Bessa wasn't Catholic." Alex rubbed the urn.

"When is everyone coming over?" Letti hopped off the chair and grabbed an apple from a bowl on the island.

"Next Saturday," Alex said.

"Whose year is it to take Mom?" Lukas looked at Alex.

"Why is it my job to keep track of this?" She pointed to

the basket.

Lukas grabbed her a perfect honeycrisp and pretended to toss it underhand. "It's not."

Alex held out her index finger out and start the count, "We had her the first year, Jens the second, then Nora. Did Nora keep it two years?"

"Does it matter?" Letti rolled her eyes. "Let them fight over it. Or we keep her and you hide her in my closet again, which is creepy, Mom."

Letti bolted through the door. "I'm doing my paper on burials," she hollered, and the dogs barked until they realized it was only her.

"Puck, down." She skipped past the dogs and sat next to Alex. She waved at the urn. "Hi Bessa. How was your day?" Then she gave Alex a smirk. "How was your day, Mom?"

"We sat here today and contemplated what to get your father for his birthday. I was thinking a new speaker for the barn, Bessa thought fainting goats would be fun."

"Dad hates goats."

"Wait. A paper on burials. Where did that come from?"

"Gee, I wonder. I asked around today what people wanted done with their remains when they died and what they did with their relatives."

A little mortified, Alex stared at her daughter. "I thought we were done with this. The neighbors will talk."

"Oh, don't worry. Most people enjoy talking about this." Letti pulled out her notebooks from her backpack. "The lady at the library said her mama was buried in the cemetery up the hill right next to her daddy. But Dusty's wife won't bury him there because she doesn't like Mama at all. Dusty's her brother. Died from a bad liver. She's going to take him to Fort Logan, where he can have a military funeral. The dogs are under her tree out back, but her husband can't bear to put Buster under the ground yet, it'll probably be another year before they get him planted. She said it's not like fish where you can flush 'em. She was glad they didn't have horses or anything. She didn't even know what you'd do with them, except make glue. That's when I stopped her." Letti looked at toward the pasture. "Too close with Lily and Tink."

Alex patted Letti on the back. "You never had a chance at being normal with mine and your Daddy's genes. God help us."

"One of my teachers wants her remains planted under a tree. One that has pink flowers in the spring. Dylan said I'm crazy. He's jelly that I picked a fun subject instead of something boring."

"Well, that's not a nice thing to say about your boyfriend."

"He's not my boyfriend. He's writing about the traffic lights in town."

Alex nodded. "Boring."

"What do you want done with you when you die, Mom?"

Alex paused.

"Is something wrong?" Letti's body tensed.

Alex giggled, "You really want to know? It's kinda morbid and your father doesn't like it."

"Give it to me."

"I want to go to a body farm."

"What is that?" Letti asked while typing something into her phone.

Instead of answering her question, Alex waited. She figured her daughter was looking up body farm.

Letti cringed. "That's gross!" She showed Alex a picture

of rotting human legs in shallow water.

Alex pushed the phone away. "Just because I want to donate my body to a farm, doesn't mean I want to look at the pictures. They have a place in Grand Junction that takes bodies. By knowing what happens to a body during decomposition, it can help law enforcement solve crimes."

"You mean rotting bodies." Letti tried to show Alex another picture of a body inside the trunk of a car.

"I don't want to be in anything."

"It's not like you can breathe anymore, anyway."

Lukas tromped into the house. The dogs barked again. "Who can't breathe?"

"Mom's dead body in a trunk at a body farm."

"What is wrong with you two?" He stomped away toward the back of the house.

"Wait. What do you want done with your body when you die, Daddy?"

"Burn me, take my ashes up to Granby during the winter. Take that trail that will lead you up as high as you can go. Drink a beer. Toss me to the wind."

Letti stuck out her tongue. "I don't like beer. I don't want to be cremated. It produces too many toxins."

Lukas sat and put his face on the table. "So does cow shit, but we need it for fertilizer. We are not talking about your death, Letti. If I have to bury you, they will need to bury me. New subject."

Alex leaned toward the urn, "Bessa and I were trying to decide what we should get you for your birthday today, got any ideas for us?"

"A new fishing rod." Lukas answered. "And a trip with my girls to the lake. I can go up on Friday and you two can come up on Saturday and spend the night."

"Ugh," Alex said.

"Mom, you're such a wussy."

"I hate camping."

"That's all I want for my birthday. Is a day away with my girls," Lukas said.

Alex opened her calendar. "Okay, but we're not going until June. I'm not going camping when it's cold."

"Deal," Lukas said.

"How about Father's Day weekend?"

He gasped. "Really? Will you two come up on that Friday with me? That can be my Father's Day present too."

Alex squeezed Lukas' shoulder. "You're her father not mine. She can go up an extra night and I will come up on Saturday."

Letti hugged Lukas. "Fine by me. We can do some night fishing."

Alex's phone chimed. It was Nora. "Hello?"

"Is Lukas there?" She asked.

"Yes," Alex said.

"Put me on speaker," Nora demanded.

Alex tapped her phone and told her, "Okay. Go. Wait. Letti is here."

"Oh, my God! I'm looking at Nancy's page." Nora said.

Lukas pushed up the sleeves on his shirt. "Get off your social media site and quit being a—what do you call it Letti?"

Letti giggled. "Creeper. Stalker."

"Yeah, that," Lukas said.

She wrote. "If they make a monster out of you because you walked away from their drama, so be it. Let them deal with what they've created. Be at peace with yourself and stay out of the conflict. -Dodinsky. And Aunt Else liked it? Why the hell is Aunt Else talking to her, anyway?"

Alex informed Lukas, "Because you all won't talk to

Aunt Else. So she talks to Nancy."

Letti took out her phone and said. "I think it's comical how adults tell us to mind our own business when they spend more time creeping on other people's social media. Who cares what Nancy says and who cares if Aunt Else likes it?"

"It's not right. Dad's sister should be on our side, not hers."

Letti whispered, "Drama, drama, drama." She spoke louder. "Auntie Nora, what do you want us to do with your body when you die?"

"Hmm. Not sure."

"You better figure it out, or we'll put you in the purple urn with Bessa." Letti winked at her parents. "Love you guys, I'm going to Dylan's." She grabbed her keys and started for the door.

"Is his mom home?" Nora asked.

"Probably. Love you, Auntie Nora."

"You shouldn't let her go over there if his parents aren't home," Nora said.

"I'm not sure what's worse. Creeping on Nancy's social media sites or telling us how to raise our daughter," Lukas said.

"You'll be sorry." Nora said.

"Just because you were doing guys in the basement, doesn't mean Letti will." Lukas said in the smart-ass tone he saved for his sister.

"That was Jens." Nora objected.

"Oh, that's right. You got caught behind the pizza place in town, by Mom. What is it you were doing back there again?"

Nora hung up on them.

Alex smacked Lukas. "You're so mean."

28. THE TENTH LETTER. ENOUGH IS ENOUGH!

"How's ole T-Bone the—" Jens strolled into the room with Desiree, who was dressed for a fashion show in Paris instead of a Sunday dinner in Rowley, Colorado.

Nora covered Julia's ears. "Jens, why do you have to be such a jerk?" She spun her oldest child around, led her to the sliding glass door, and then onto the deck outside.

Alex was still irritated that Jens and Desiree were back together. She was too young. And even if Jens hadn't figured it out, Alex knew Beth was the one for him. Fran was certain of this too, but told Alex to stay out of it. She had said, "If it's meant to be, it will be." Alex wasn't about to take a chance on that.

Desiree found her way to Letti. Probably because Letti was the closest to her age. "Hi, Letti, how's school?"

Letti answered. "It's good, almost done for the year."

"You'll be a junior next year, right? How exciting."

"I'm excited for summer."

"What activities are you involved in?"

"I'm part of the Teen Library Council for the county."

"Is that fun? Do you like reading books?"

Alex moved in and put her hand on Desiree's back. "Letti reads hundreds of books a year. We begged her to go to the library more because we couldn't afford her habit. Can I get you something to drink?"

"Bottled water?" Desiree asked.

"Cold or room temp?"

"Room temp is fine, thank you."

Alex grabbed a bottled water from the pantry. "So tell me what's new. Any word on the commercial?"

"Didn't you see it? It's been airing since February," Desiree followed Alex into the kitchen.

"I did, but I thought there were more," Alex said. Per Jens request, they all watched the ad for a prescription drug that helped people sleep—several times.

Nora grabbed a glass out of the cupboard and filled it with tap water. She walked over to Letti. "What are you reading? Anything good that I might like?"

"The Guernsey Literary and Potato Peel Society. It's amazing."

Nora scrunched her nose and showed her teeth. "I watched the movie last week."

"You didn't like it?" Letti asked.

"Loved it," Nora said. "But I can't read a book once I've seen the movie."

"Me neither," Letti said.

"I'd rather watch the movie," Desiree said.

"Too superficial." Nora said.

"Supper's ready," Lukas called out.

After everyone finished their burgers and they tossed the paper plates, the entire family remained on the main level of the house. Since there were only a few more letters, they all agreed to keep everyone together. Travis tried to use

Rowan as an excuse to go outside, but Nora wouldn't allow it. "Two more letters. You can sit with us."

Alex moved the urn to the center of the dining room table and took out the tenth letter from the drawer in the hutch, "Are we ready?"

Nora's voice was soft. "No."

"Enough is enough," Alex said.

Nora huffed. "Are you being bossy? Or is that the title of the letter?" Her eyes crossed.

Alex displayed the purple envelope so she could see the writing scrolled on it.

Enough is enough!

"Postmarked, Rowley, Colorado," Alex said. "I give up. I have no idea who is sending these. Who's taking her this year?"

Jens wiggled in his seat. "It's my turn, but Desiree and I are going on a cruise, and then we won't be home much with me working and her on set. She's starting a new shoot in a couple of weeks."

"It's not like she needs babysitting. Not you, Desiree. Mama." Nora's voice was sharp and cold, "She's dead." She covered her mouth. "I'm sorry. I didn't mean it that way."

Letti added her two cents. "She's dead. Ashes. Dead. And it's weird you pass that thing around like it's her. Really, y'all should bury her."

Jens sat up straight. "No. It's okay. I'll take her this year."

Lukas rubbed his forehead, "It's not like she wants to be kept for another year. We need to decide what to do."

Letti grabbed the envelope, "I'm reading this year. Any objections?" Letti pulled out the paper and raised his left eyebrow. "Anyone needing a potty break better go now. This one is long."

Desiree took a deep breath in.

"Kidding," Letti giggled. "Okay, hush family."

Hello, my sweet and most amazing family. Are you still doing this? What is wrong with you? Alex, are you enjoying this? We always had a fun time watching the three of them, didn't we?

Alex chuckled a little and winked at Letti.

Seriously though, I'm dead. Remains stuffed in a beautiful urn that I picked out. Well, Letti and I picked out.

"I was little. I don't remember. I would've picked the pink one now. But, yes, you are dead."

The urn is probably on my kitchen table while the six, wait, probably the seven of you gather. I'm sure my little Letti is here too, all grown up and braver than the rest of you.

"She was smart, wasn't she?" Letti said.

Thank your parents. I'm sure neither of them will coddle you, but the love they will shower on you will be quite amazing.

"They're okay." Letti elbowed Lukas and Alex.

Lukas, my son, I love you. I'm sure you're still the best daddy in the world.

Letti raised her left eyebrow. "You kinda are, Daddy."

Do what you always do and take charge. Get rid of the contents in that purple jar; those ashes are not me. I'm counting on you.

Nora, are your kids sitting with you? I'm sure you have them. Nora, my protector. You will go out of your way to keep your family safe. How many do you have now, three? Four? Don't let anyone tell you you're not parenting correctly. If they do, smile and say, "Thank you. I don't think I asked for your opinion."

Nora added, "Or, kiss my ass, I didn't ask for your opinion."

"I'm still surprised your children don't have your

mouth," Jens stood, picked up his nephew and ruffled his hair.

Travis told on his son. "Eli was sent to the principal's office last week for calling his friend a jackass."

"You must be so proud," Jens said.

Nora flipped him the bird.

Eli copied his mother.

Jens put his own hand over Eli's. "Don't be bad like your mama. Be a good boy like your Uncle Jens."

Nora kept her middle finger flying.

But seriously, make sure they aren't completely protected. A little adversity is good. Obviously, I wasn't talking about me when I said you didn't need other opinions. I love you, my sweet girl.

Jenny Boy, are you still working too hard? Are you married yet? Or is some young twenty something sitting next to you?

A second of silence can sometimes last too long. Alex knew this, but she didn't know what to say. She nudged Letti, who continued to read.

Yep, I went there. It's fine. As long as she's nice and she's real. If she's not, it will never work. Trust me.

Sorry I went there again, and only when I'm talking to you. But you've always been my favorite. Yes, I said that, too.

Letti argued. "Hey, I thought I was her favorite."

Jens replied, "I tried to tell you this a long time ago, kid. You wouldn't listen."

Don't any of you get in a tizzy over this. Jenny was always the one who loved me most. Mama's boy from the beginning and I'm sure he'll be with me when I pass. He will not let go of me easily. He will be the first to fight it.

A tear fell onto Jens' cheek, but what should have been more noticeable was Desiree missing.

You all need to figure out what you want to do with

me. I don't care what it is. Hopefully you already have, but I've given you ten years to do it. Now you have thirty days, yes DAYS to decide. If you haven't, the next purple envelope has a solution. It will arrive on day twenty-nine. I expect that my wishes will be granted if you all can't agree.

I love you all with everything I have at this moment while I'm alive. Remember, my love for you is eternal; these ashes are not.

Yours for eternity,

Mom/Mama

P.S. Magnus also knows what I really want. But that's not what I have written down. Tell him it's never too late. And if that is the solution, then my wishes on day twenty-nine won't matter anymore.

Jens stood. "What the—? Why would dad know what she wants? Cheating bastard doesn't know a damn thing. We need to find out who is sending these and get the next letter now."

"Okay, Sherlock. You get on that," Lukas got up from the table.

"Obviously only Grandpa really knows what she wants. Which is weird if you ask me, but ask him." Letti pushed the letter to the middle of the table.

Nora picked it up and scanned through it, "She wants us to agree on something. We need to try. This is the last thing she's asked us to do."

Jens headed for the front door. "I need time to think about this. I also need to find Desiree. I'll call you." He squeezed Alex on the forearm. "Thanks for dinner."

Alex followed him to the door and gave him a hug. She held on a little longer before he pulled away. It's what Bessa would have done.

Once he was in his car, Lukas said, "We really need to find him someone."

Letti giggled. "He already found her. He's just too stupid to realize it."

Lukas asked Letti. "Who?"

"Beth. Duh."

Alex pushed her husband on the shoulder with hers, "Yeah, duh!"

Lukas put his arm around Letti. "You girls think you know everything. Are we going to read your letter out loud?"

"Nope. I already read it. You guys can read it. I'm meeting Dylan at the library."

"It's family day." Lukas argued.

"Jens left."

"She is right," Alex said.

Lukas shrugged. "Fine. Go."

My Sweetest Letti,

What would I tell my 17-year-old self? Letti, I would tell her nothing. Nothing at all. Because every decision, right or wrong, brought me three wonderful children and you. If I changed anything or told myself anything, there could be a possibility of changing what I have now. I had relationships that didn't work out; I let some good ones go. I didn't spend enough time with some people, and I spent too much time with some that didn't deserve my time. It still brought me the best life.

Okay, maybe one thing I'd tell myself. Use sunscreen on your neck and hands.

That's it. Except I love you. And really, you are my favorite human. Don't tell Jens.

Forever,

Your Bessa

29. AND HE FOUND HIS NUTS AGAIN

Build your own BLT's is always a hit unless you're a vegan. None of them were vegans. However, being in the meat industry, Alex was a food snob. Travis filled cups with milk for the kids. "Isn't this stuff six dollars a gallon?"

"Yep," Alex shut the refrigerator door behind him.

"What happens if you don't buy organic? I mean seriously, my kids do just fine with the cheaper milk."

Alex placed lids on the cups. "I'm sure they do. Remember this day when the girls start their periods and get boobs early. All those hormones in your cheap milk will give you those added benefits. Your boys may even get man boobs." Alex plucked the top of his shirt with her fingers. "Do you have man boobs?"

"Will they really get boobs early? Periods?" He froze. "Lukas, do something with your wife."

Lukas peeked into the house from the porch, "I've tried."

Once all the kids had their food and settled at the picnic table in the backyard, the adults eyed the bacon. Alex covered the plate with a paper towel. "As soon as your brother gets here, we can eat."

Travis pouted. "Who put him in charge of picking up Magnus?"

"My wife," Lukas answered.

"It was a good idea. It gives them time to talk," Alex said. The dogs started barking and Alex looked out the window. "Shit."

"Shit, what?" Lukas asked.

Alex raced out on the back deck. "Letti, keep the kids out here, okay. When they're done, have them play out here or in the basement."

"Okay?"

"Trust me." Alex said before slogging back into the house,

The front door flew open and Jens stomped in like a spoiled child who hadn't gotten his way. "I give up."

There was a knock on the door behind him. Alex stood in place. "I'm not answering it; he's your dad." She brushed her hands together and headed to the urn. "God help us."

Travis moved closer to Alex. "Not mine either. I'm hanging with no-hormone-lady."

Lukas walked to the door. "Really, Dad? Today of all days? This was about healing our family."

Nancy's voice echoed through the house. "I'm part of your father's life. If healing happens, we ALL need to heal."

Alex stayed put next to Nora and Travis by the table, watching Nancy physically shake.

Travis stood behind Nora, pressing his hands on her arms. He squeezed and rubbed. "We can go."

Nora took a deep breath, rubbed his left hand and said, "No. I have a better idea." She turned to the urn and picked it up. She hugged it. "Let's do this, Mama." She strode with her head held high to the dining room. As she passed the door she said, “Oh good, you’re here, Daddy. We we’re going to sit down with Mama and discuss where her ashes should go. She told us in a letter that you knew. She also said that when she died, you were still the love of her life.” She set the urn in the middle of the table, looking at it lovingly, and then peeked behind her to the front door. “Oh, Nancy. I didn’t know you were coming. This is a private time with our mom, I’m sure you understand.”

Nancy’s entire face became red, and her eyes bulged out like a pug. “Magnus, I’m not doing this. They need to treat me with respect.”

“This, from the slut who broke up a thirty-year marriage.” Jens said.

“I won’t—” she started to say something and then crossed her arms and stomped away like a child.

“You did.” Jens reminded her.

Letti opened the sliding door and peeked into the kitchen. “The kids want to come in.”

Nancy pulled out a cloth from her pocket and blotted at the tear on her cheek. She waved at Letti, “Come give Granny and Papa a hug goodbye.”

Letti closed the door.

Nancy’s breathing got heavier, like she was birthing a child. “See what you kids have done? I love that girl and have done so much for her. I’m really the only grandmother she knows. I’ve loved her more than the other two grandmas combined and now she won’t even talk to me. What have you told her?”

“Oh, no you don’t.” Alex marched to the entrance to the house. “Bessa loved my daughter more than you could imagine. My mother loves Letti more than that. Don’t you ever walk into my home and demand anything.” Alex opened the front door. "Time for you to go." She glared at Magnus, "If you can find your balls, you can stay."

The three siblings choked.

Magnus helped Nancy out. She wailed to the point of hyperventilating.

"Always the victim." Alex slammed the door behind them.

Lukas, Nora, and Jens stood still and quiet.

"I'm done," Alex hissed. Her tone changed, her voice loud but sweet. "Kids, you can come in now." And of course, because they could, they didn't.

Out front, tires kicked up rocks, and the car peeled out of the driveway. A few seconds later, the front door opened. Magnus stood alone. "I hope you all are happy. I chose you over her today, and it will cost me."

"Sounds like she's still in control of your nuts, Pops." Jens strolled passed him into the kitchen.

Magnus followed. "Why do you always have to be such a little prick?"

"Mine isn't little." Jens grabbed four glasses out of the cupboard.

"Nice one," Magnus said.

Nora took each glass and filled them with crushed ice from the refrigerator door. She placed them back on the island while Lukas grabbed the bottle of vodka from the freezer and poured the clear liquid. Magnus took a lemon from the fruit bowl and Nora handed him a cutting board and knife. He cut the lemon into wedges and added one to three glasses. He handed the glass missing the lemon to Jens, and the other to Nora and Lukas. Magnus lifted his glass. "Skol," he said, and they drank.

Alex snorted. She laughed out loud, which ended up in a cry. "I wish I had recorded that."

"Recorded what?" Lukas asked.

"It's amazing how synced you are—but not."

Lukas took another gulp and said, "I'm hungry." He grabbed a plate and handed it to Magnus, "We're doing make-your-own BLT's."

Alex interrupted, "I also have a salad."

"Thank you, I'd rather have a BLT," Magnus said.

"You should probably stay away from the bacon with your condition." Jens handed Magnus a bowl.

Magnus waved him off. "I don't want another damn salad."

"Daddy," Nora said.

"What?" Magnus said.

"The kids," she said.

"I don't see any kids."

Letti stood at the top of the stairs. "Right here, Grandpa." She raised her hand.

"You're not a kid. You have boobs now," Magnus corrected her.

"Oh. My. Gawd." Letti tramped back down the stairs. "What is wrong with you people?"

"Dad," Lukas said.

"Facts of life. Girls grow up. They get boobs." Magnus put four slices of bacon on the top of his bread and picked up the jar from the counter. "What the hell is vegenaise?"

Travis chimed in, "Your daughter-in-law is all healthy and organic. So I'm sure it's some weird version of mayo."

Lukas took the knife out of the jar and tried to help Magnus with his sandwich. "Try it before you complain."

Magnus grabbed another couple pieces of bacon and layered them on top of what he already had. "I can make my damn sandwich."

"Daddy, do you think you should eat that much?" Nora reached over and tried to grab some bacon off his sandwich.

Magnus set the plate down, "You let me drink vodka, you made bacon, and now you want to tell me I can't eat it. I'm not two. I didn't complain about the damn mayonnaise, I only wanted to know what it was. Now get the hell out of my way."

"And he's found his nuts again," Jens said while putting another piece of bacon on his father's plate. "Now, are you going to tell us what Mom wants done with her ashes, or not?"

Magnus put the plate down. "Or not. I can't do this right now." He shuffled down the stairs.

30. HERE YOU GO, A WOMAN IS IN THE ROOM.

Alex took a plane home from LA a day early. She didn't want to get stuck in California because of the bomb cyclone heading to Colorado. She headed to the grocery store after picking up the water jugs at the house. She watched people shop while she filled the containers at the water dispenser in the back of the store. It was interesting what people would put in their carts when the snow was coming.

Alex had made a meal plan and a list of groceries on the plane to cover her family for three days. Even if they were socked in, the Colorado sun would melt the heaviest of blizzards enough for them to get out. They wouldn't starve. She had plenty of food in the house. It was produce she needed more than anything.

Dinner - Fish Tacos

Breakfast - Eggs, Bacon, Fruit

Lunch - Reuben sandwiches with homemade Russian Dressing

Dinner - Chicken Soup

Breakfast - Biscuits and Gravy

Lunch - Leftover Chicken Soup

Dinner - Jambalaya

Breakfast - Breakfast Burritos

Lunch - Leftover Jambalaya (on their own if we are not snowed in)

Dinner - Eating out anywhere! If we are still snowed in, people will have to look for the bodies.

Shortly after she arrived back at the house with all the necessities, the rain turn to snow. Lukas' truck sat in the open garage, but Letti wasn't home yet. Alex pulled in next to Lukas' truck and sat in her car. She grabbed her phone and started to text Letti, but called her instead.

Letti answered after two rings. "Hi Mom."

"Should you be talking and driving?" A man's voice said over the speaker.

"Who's with you?"

"Grandpa."

"Magnus?"

"Yes."

"Right here. She's an excellent driver, our Letti. I've been staying with Nora, but with the snow coming, I don't think I can be stuck in that house with all those kids. Damn it. Don't tell Nora I said that. I told her I wanted to see Letti for a few days. Which is true, Letti, I want to see you. I also don't want to be cooped up in a house with all those little ones."

"You picked us because Uncle Jens said no. Nice try, Grandpa."

"Watch the road."

"Now you sound like Grandmother."

"Where are you?" Alex asked.

"Next to the vet," Letti said.

Alex checked the time on her phone. They were only about five minutes away. "I'm hanging up. Drive safe."

Alex got out of the car and zipped up her coat. The wind was picking up, and the snow swirled in the driveway. She popped the trunk and grabbed the three reusable bags and took them into the house. Lukas sat at the table looking at his computer. The dogs barked, Bishop ran in circles around Alex, and Puck clawed at the back of her legs.

"Stop. No." She put the bags on the counter and put her hand out toward Puck. "Sit." Once the dog obeyed, she petted her. "You're a pain in the ass. But I love you."

"Love you, too." Lukas said, still looking at the screen of his computer.

Alex sauntered over to see what was so interesting. She kissed him and then looked at the screen. "Did you join a social media site?"

"Yep. I already have sixty-two friends. This shit is weird." He scrolled through the page. "The county is already on Accident Alert. Have you talked to Letti?"

"She should be home any minute. Did you have something you forgot to tell me?"

He stood. "No. Do you have more in the car?"

"Yes. Can you help me with the water?"

"Yep."

She followed him to the garage. "You didn't tell me about your dad."

"Nothing to tell. He's with Nora, thank God."

Alex snorted.

"What?" He moved the bottles out of the car and stacked them on a wooden shelf he'd built when they moved in.

"Oh, nothing." She paced back into the house and checked out the clock on the range. Instead of fretting about Letti, she put the groceries away.

Still no Letti.

She looked out the window in the laundry room and the

only change to the driveway was more snow. She opened the washer to see if Lukas or Letti left anything to mold while she'd been away. It was empty. She opened the dryer. It was also empty. She rearranged cleaners on the shelves so that like items were with like items, combined bottles of window cleaner, and tossed empty bottles into the recycling bin

Still no Letti.

Finally, after twenty-five minutes, Letti's car slowly drove into the third bay of the garage—the benefit of being an only child. Alex opened the laundry room door to the garage and stood with her hands on her hips.

Letti jumped out of the car and tattled on her grandfather. "He made me go to the store." She grabbed his suitcase from the trunk.

Magnus rolled himself out of the car holding several plastic bags. He lifted them. "I needed some snacks. I also thought I'd make lamb for dinner tomorrow."

When Letti got to the door, Alex hugged her tight. "Thank God, you're safe. I love you."

"I didn't die, Mom"

"Wow." Alex said.

Letti hugged Alex back. "Love you too, Mom." Letti filed into the kitchen and dropped the suitcase next to the tall table. "Dad is on social media?"

"What took you so long?" Lukas asked.

"Your father."

"What?"

Still holding the garage door open for Magnus, Alex peeked into the kitchen. Lukas shut his laptop, noticed the suitcase Letti had, and took a step back when Magnus sauntered in. "I knew I should have gone to confession last week. Is this my punishment?" Lukas said.

"Damn it," Magnus said. "Do you have crackers?" He

searched one bag before setting it on the island. "I got herring, but I need saltines."

"I have crackers," Alex said.

"I friend requested you, Dad." Letti held up her phone. She stepped back and lowered her phone. "On second thought, no."

"What do you mean, no?" Lukas asked.

"I don't need you posting weird crap on my page. Auntie Nora is bad enough," she said.

"What is posting?" Magnus asked.

Alex took the food out of the bags Magnus brought in and put them on the counter. Two cans of smoked herring in natural juice. "Nasty."

"What's nasty?" Magnus asked.

She held up one of the two jars from the bag, "Fillets in cream sauce." She rummaged through the bag, "Herring in Paprika Cream, Herring in Dill Herb Sauce. Smoked herring in natural juice, what is natural juice? Never mind, I don't want to know."

"Don't knock it until you've tried it," Magnus said.

Letti showed Magnus a picture on her phone. "This is posting."

Alex tried to look at the post. "What did you write?"

Letti showed Magnus the picture of Alex she had just taken and posted with Alex's scrunched face.

He squinted and read aloud, "Grandpa brought fish in a jar. Nasty!"

"Where is that?"

"Online, Grandpa,"

"How did you get that online so fast?"

"Social media, Grandpa,"

"I think Nancy does that."

"How long are you staying, Dad?" Lukas asked. "You've

got enough canned fish to last a month."

"I thought I'd get extra for you, I'm sure you don't go shopping much."

Alex stuck up for Lukas. "While this is true, it's not because Lukas won't, I don't let him. He'd come home with a bunch of junk." She took out two packages of ice cream sandwiches. "Like this."

"Exactly," Magnus said.

WITHIN A FEW HOURS, the sheriff closed the state highway into town. Lukas stayed glued to his computer, occasionally trying to get others to look at pictures from across the county. "Vehicles are stuck everywhere," he said. "Maybe I should go out in the truck and help."

"And get stuck too? I don't think so." Alex said.

Alex put the cod into the oven, started the rice, and was making homemade spicy avocado ranch dressing for the coleslaw to put on top of the tacos. "How spicy do you like things?" she asked Magnus.

"He's a wuss." Lukas said without looking up from his computer screen.

She kept the dressing mild and cut up jalapeños on the side for Letti, and herself. The reality was Lukas was just as much as a wuss as his father with spicy food.

They sat together in the dining room at the table Magnus and Bessa had purchased the year they moved into the house. Alex watched Magnus smooth his hand over the worn wood. "She loved this table."

"Yep," Lukas filled his corn taco with rice and fish before passing the food to Alex.

She lifted her head toward Magnus. "You all get yours first."

Magnus didn't look up. "You were four years old, Nora was three and Jens was barely one. She wanted a table. A big table. Where one day we could all sit." He swallowed. "Together. She knew the second she saw it, she wanted it. She said it was sturdy. She said she wouldn't have to worry if you all banged it up. You guys did everything on this table. Homework, Christmas cookies, board games." He choked out the last, "The best family dinners."

Lukas took Magnus' plate. "Wait until you try these fish tacos Alex made."

After dinner, Lukas got back onto his computer and Letti and Magnus cleaned up the kitchen. Alex disappeared to the bedroom to unpack. Dirty clothes in the hamper, makeup back in the bathroom drawers, and her printed sale material in the suitcase to go back downstairs into her office. She rolled the suitcase down the hall and found Letti and Magnus at the dining room table, pulling out the cribbage board.

"Who taught you how to play. Letti?" Magnus asked.

"Bessa."

Alex peeked at Letti's hand. "I play the winner. She was taught from the best, so you better play tough, Magnus. She will take your missed points too. My guess is you'll be watching the next game."

Alex snuck up on Lukas who sat with his faced shoved into the computer screen. She stared at him and waited for him to notice her. When he finally noticed her, she put her hand on her hip. "Really? Now I'm going to have to compete for your attention too? You've had your face in that thing all night except for dinner, which you slammed down."

"That's not true."

"What time is it?" Alex placed her hand on the screen clock so he couldn't see the time.

"Seven at the latest."

She removed her hand. "Try eight thirty."

Lukas closed his computer.

After everything was in its place, Alex returned to find Lukas, Letti, and Magnus all sitting at the table, along with the urn. Letti was in the lead. "She's gonna whoop your ass."

Magnus studied his cards. "We're playing two out of three, two out of three." Magnus said.

"I think that's a great idea, I'm hitting the sack, if that's okay with all of you. I've had a long week at work."

Magnus blew her a kiss. "Sleep well, love. Thank you for dinner."

ALEX WOKE TO HER DOG, Puck, nestled against her feet, and clanging of pots and pans in the kitchen. Tense voices argued over how to cook bacon. Outside the window, the snow flew, and she wasn't able to see Pikes Peak in the distance. She rolled out of bed, washed her face, brushed her hair and teeth, and changed into sweats.

Puck followed Alex out of the bedroom and down the hall. "There better be boiling water for my tea since you two woke me up," she scolded the men.

Lukas and Magnus stood at the island over two packages of bacon. Magnus held one up. "First, I've never seen a bacon package this small. Second, Lukas wants to put it on a pan in the oven. Tell him that's ridiculous."

Lukas handed Alex her mug with a tea bag and boiling water.

"Sugar?" Alex asked.

"Yep. Already in," Lukas answered.

"Thank you." She poured heavy cream into the mug,

stirred it with a spoon, and took a long drink. "Perfect. It's only taken us eighteen years to train each other."

"Ha ha." Lukas shared with his father, "I do it mostly perfect. Margaret makes the perfect cup of tea, I come in a close second."

"Letti." Alex took the bacon out of Magnus' hand. "First, whoever makes my tea, wins. Second, we only need one of these. It's not small, its packaged differently." She placed the extra package back in the refrigerator. "Third, I always cook the bacon in the oven. Less grease spatter and evenly cooked makes perfect slices; not ridiculous. Now shoo out of the kitchen, old man."

Lukas lifted his coffee mug to his father, "Skol." Lukas took a drink of his coffee. After setting the mug down, he placed the strips of bacon evenly on the pan.

"Did you know bacon comes from pigs stomach?" Magnus asked.

Alex schooled her father-in-law. "Bacon is not from the stomach. They cut it from the belly portion of the pig, That's why it has so much fat on it. And probably why you shouldn't be eating it."

"Dad, she's been in the meat business for years. But if you'd been around, you would have known."

Alex pointed at the clock on the microwave. "No fighting before noon." She looked out the window, to the huge drifts along the fence in the backyard. "We will be stuck in this house for," she paused. "How long, do you think?" she asked Lukas.

"At least today. Maybe most of tomorrow," he said.

"So, if the two of you plan on hashing it out, which I think is a good thing, you can't start until after one in the afternoon, and it has to stop by dinner. Got it?"

Magnus grabbed the second pack of bacon out of the

fridge. "If you make the second pack, it's a deal."

Alex yanked it out of his hand. "You're lucky you're getting any bacon. Had I known you were coming, meal planning for the next few days would have been different. I don't need you dying here in this blizzard. Now put the bacon back and get out of my kitchen. Both of you. Wait, Lukas, you can stay and help me."

Alex heard stomping in the garage and then the door to the laundry room opened. Letti appeared, all bundled up. "Girls are safe in the barn. They've been fed, and the water hasn't frozen. I'm going back to bed."

"Aren't you hungry?" Magnus asked.

"Save me bacon, please. I'm taking advantage of the snow day. Going back to bed." She shuffled back to her room like she just woke.

Magnus watched her stumble down the hall. "I'd be awake after going out in the cold."

Alex, Lukas, and Magnus sat at the table. Lukas was the one who put everything in the dining room instead of the table between the kitchen and family room he, Alex, and Letti normally sat at.

"Am I allowed to put some herring on my plate?" Magnus asked like a five-year-old asking for ice cream. Alex had plated his food so he wouldn't eat too much bacon.

"Yep." Alex said. "I put it all in the pantry. Want me to get it for you?"

"Nope, I've got it." While in the pantry looking for it he asked, "Who eats the sardines?"

Alex hollered back. "I do. I know you can't believe it. But like herring they are fantastic for you and they don't taste all salty and fishy like yours do."

"Mind if I try them?"

"Go for it."

"She eats them with peaches and jalapeños in the summer." Lukas curled his lip and made a gagging noise.

Magnus brought the can of fish back to the table and opened it. He put a fillet on his plate and took a bite. "Not bad. I would do the peaches, but not the peppers." He picked up the can. "Anyone?"

After Alex and Lukas shook their heads, he piled the rest on his plate.

IF ALEX HAD KNOWN they would start at one sharp, she would have downloaded a boxing bell to her phone. Lukas, Letti, and Magnus finished watching one of the new Star Wars movies while Alex answered emails for work.

When the final credits began, Lukas opened fire. "The only reason you're talking to us is because Nancy kicked you out."

"When did I stop talking to you?"

"Which time? We can fast forward to Nora's wedding." Lukas said.

"That's not true."

"Texts with thumbs up doesn't count as talking, Dad."

"I went to little Julia's birthday."

"Oh, okay. How old is Julia now?"

Magnus didn't answer that question. "Letti came over few months ago, right Letti?"

"I'm glad you still talk to your granddaughter, but until your heart attack, we have not seen each other since I told your wife, 'I didn't give a rats ass about her Christmas at Granny's.' She's not Letti's Granny and she sure as hell isn't my mother."

"She loves Letti, doesn't she, Letti?" Magnus looked at her.

"I'm out." Letti grabbed her phone and water before standing. She took a few snacks out of the pantry before disappearing to her room. The dogs followed.

"There you go, Dad."

"You two keep Letti out of your bullshit." Alex looked up from her computer. "I get a day at home with family and you guys start and she disappears."

"We've texted." Magnus said.

"That's your response? Okay. I'll play that game. I have all of our text since Nora's wedding. Want to go through them together? There are 72 texts. I've counted. Several times. 42 from me and 30 from you. All of yours are in response to mine. And 11 of those are a thumb-up picture. Want to look at them?"

Alex closed her computer and slipped away.

"Don't leave," Magnus pleaded. "We need a woman in the room to keep the peace."

Alex stomped over to the dining room table, grabbed the urn and stomped back. She placed it on the table, looking over them. "Here you go, a woman is in the room." She left them alone and walked back to Letti's room and knocked on the door.

"Come in."

Alex entered. She shut the door behind her. "Can I sit?"

Letti tapped on the mattress.

Alex scanned the room. It wasn't bad. She grabbed a pillow from the end of the bed and set it behind her. She wiggled in to get comfy. "You okay?"

"I'm fine," Letti said.

"You know, just because we have all this crap going on, doesn't mean you have to play in any of it. You can like who you like, love who you love, and tell the rest of us to pound sand as your Daddy would say."

"Nancy actually drives me crazy. She uses me to get to the rest of you. She doesn't even know me. I know they give me money every Christmas and birthday. She sends it, signs the card, Love Granny and Papa. But the actual truth lies with how she acts, what she does."

"Has she said something?"

"No. It's not what she says, it's what she doesn't say." Letti grabbed her phone and opened an app. She put her phone to her chest. "Before I show you this, I want you to know I don't care. I'm not hurt. Social Media does not define me, Mom."

Alex looked up on the wall at the sign she had a friend make for Letti. "Social Media does not define who I am. I define who I am."

"Okay," Alex said.

Letti handed Alex her phone. "Scroll through."

It was Nancy's page. "She's out of control," Letti said. "Sometimes I unfollow her because I don't want to see it. Besides all the political posts, she posts all about her grandkids and how much she loves them and how beautiful they are. On days I visit. There is nothing." Letti held out her hand.

Alex placed the phone in it. "I'm sure she–"

"Stop, mom. I don't care. But for them to act like she *loves me so much*, it's stupid and a lie. When I go there, I want to see Grandpa, but he doesn't talk much. He pays more attention to the television and ignores both of us. If I can get him when he's working in the shop, and she's not around, it's great. But if she's there, she steals the show. She talks, talks, talks. About all the things she's doing. Her grandkids. How everyone in the world is corrupt. How she accepts everyone. That's bull all on its own. I just don't want to be in the middle anymore. I don't care what she does, who she supports, and what she thinks is important."

"It kinda sounds like you do. When we talk about things, those things seem to bother you. You don't see my dad much, but that doesn't seem to bother you," Alex said.

Letti pulled up his social media page. "Your father doesn't post anything but fishing pictures. He loves fish. That's all."

Alex took the phone and scrolled through it. "I didn't even know he had a social media page. Do you talk to him?"

"No. Do you?"

Alex handed the phone back. "No." She hadn't in years and didn't plan on starting now.

Letti clicked back to Nancy's page. "She's not my granny and I don't care." She hit the unfriend button, put down her phone, and rested her head on Alex's. "I wish I could remember Bessa."

"The tapes. I forgot about the tapes." Alex jumped off the bed, ran out of Letti's room, and to her own closet. She grabbed the handful of tapes and tapped on Letti's door, "Meet me in the living room."

Alex snapped her fingers at Lukas and Magnus sitting in the living room. "Letti and I are going to watch old tapes. If you want to continue to fight, take your asses to the basement."

She took a deep breath in and changed her tone. "Lukas, will you get the old video camera and set it up for me and Letti?"

"Now?"

"Yes, please."

"You do things at the strangest times." Lukas mocked her, but continued with the mission.

Alex sorted through the tapes. "I need to get these on a

disc or memory stick or whatever they do these days."

"What are you doing?" Magnus asked.

"I'm about ready to go down memory lane."

Letti sat next to Alex with her favorite blanket, the quilt that once belonged to Bessa.

Magnus touched the tattered piece of cloth and then looked at Letti. "Wanna hear a wonderful love story?"

"Sure?"

It was the spring of 1967 when I moved to Denver.

"From Norway?"

"No, from South Dakota. Our family traveled here from Norway by boat in 1839. Her name was Emilie."

"They named a boat?"

"Yep."

"So there are records of us at Ellis Island?"

"No."

"They traveled through the Erie Canal to the Great Lakes and settled in Wisconsin."

"Wisconsin. How can that be a wonderful love story?"

"Do you want to hear the love story or not?"

"Sure, it would be good to hear the other side of the story."

"What?" Magnus asked.

Alex tipped her head. "What are you talking about?"

"She left a book my cedar chest. I found it last year. It's called Your Grandpa and Me."

"Why didn't you share it?" Alex asked.

"I thought you knew it was there. Come on, Mom. You know everything."

Magnus relaxed on the couch. "Alex, I would love to watch the tapes with you, if you will allow me." He sat on the other side of Letti. "And I'd really love to read that story."

Letti leaned into her grandpa. "Someday, Grandpa. Someday."

JUST WHEN ALEX thought the storm had passed, the wind kicked in. Not outside, but inside the house. Outside there were three-foot drifts next to the snow fence, but the sun peeked through. Inside, the four of them watched Nora and Bessa make jam. Nora appeared to be in her late teens, early twenties.

Magnus' voice could be heard on the other side of the camera. He said, "I love apricots almost as much as I love my girls," he said. "You should put strawberries in it."

"Quit taping, Daddy. I don't have any make-up on." Nora hid her face from the camera.

Magnus wasn't on the film, but his voice was. "I'm taking Nancy Riggs on showings today." He paused. "After, I have, uh, a meeting after with another potential client looking for acreage in," he paused again, "Strasburg. So it could be a late night."

Bessa's sweet voice answered him. "No worries. I'll save you dinner."

Lukas used the remote to turn off the television. "When did you start screwing Nancy behind mom's back? Nineteen ninety-five? No wonder mom hated strawberries in her apricot jam."

Letti jerked away from her grandpa, took her blanket and said, "I'm going back to bed."

Lukas marched around the couch, away from Magnus. "I have plowing to do."

Alex stared at Magnus. "Well, I jacked that one up, didn't I?"

Magnus stood. "I'm the one who jacked that one up."

31. WHERE IS THE URN?

A few days later, after the snow melted, and Magnus left, Alex cleaned house. "Where's Bessa?" she asked Lukas.

"Again?" He looked around the living room. "Last time I saw her, she was on the kitchen table."

Alex paced toward the dining room. "She's not here."

She tapped on Letti's door.

"Come in."

Alex opened her door to find her sitting on her bed, laptop in her lap, one earbud in and one earbud out. "Have you seen Bessa?"

"Bessa is gone," Letti said matter-of-factly.

"Where?"

"She died, mom. I haven't seen her since she died. Can you please clarify? Are you talking about the urn? I'm not playing this game anymore with a glass purple kaleidoscope. The urn, not my Bessa."

"Okay. Fine. Have you seen the urn?"

"Grandpa took it to his room the other night. After him

and daddy fought. I heard him talking to it. You all talk to it too much."

"You talk to it as well."

32. I PUT MY SUGAR IN THAT. NOT ANYMORE!

Lukas handed Letti a piece of mail. "This came for me today. I thought you'd find it interesting. And it may help you with your paper."

Alex could see the envelope was from the National Cremation Society, addressed to Lukas.

"This is great." Letti sat at the table and opened it. "It's a survey. If we fill it out, they will send us a Cremation Answer Book." Letti grabbed the marker laying on the table.

"Number one:" she said. "How long have you lived at your current residence? Eleven plus years." She filled in the answer. "Number two: Have you ever been responsible for making final arrangements? Yes." She filled in the box and wrote as she talked. "Bessa hangs out in a ridiculous urn, but we've lost her. Can you help us find her? Three: how much would you expect to pay to make final arrangements?" Letti asked Lukas. "How much did it cost to cremate Bessa? Did you pay for the urn or did she?"

"She paid for it. But if we bury her, then that is not paid for."

Letti flipped the sheet of paper over. "Below two thousand. They actually have above ten thousand. Who would pay that for a funeral?"

"Rich people," Lukas said.

"Number four: in the event of your death, who would be responsible for making your funeral arrangements? Other." She giggled, "We will have to ask total strangers because my family is wack and can't make these decisions."

Letti continued to read the survey out loud. "Five: Are you aware you can make cremation arrangements in advance that will help avoid inevitable rising costs and inflation? Yes. Six: Are your loved ones and family members aware of what you desire and prefer for your final arrangements? Yes." She rolled her eyes and then mocked her dad. "Something about a beer and Grand Lake. You'd better write it down, Daddy. We might forget and put you in some weird box and pass you around. But since I'm an only child, I wouldn't want your ashes always at my house. Creepy and weird."

Lukas took the paper from Letti and held out his hand for the marker. He wrote on the back of the paper while talking, "I, Lukas Larsen, would like to be cremated and put in a cardboard box. I would like Letti and my grandchildren, if there are any, to decorate the box with crayons, and I would like to sit on Letti's mantel for as long as she'll have me."

He handed the paper back to Letti. She read it out loud and then said. "Gross. Not happening." She tossed the paper back at him. "I'm done. Are we going to Grandpa's now? I really want to get this over with."

"Yes," Lukas said. "Me too."

Alex clapped her hands together. "Come on, you two. We can do this. One dinner with Grandpa Magnus and Nancy will not kill us."

"It might," Lukas said.

Carrying in a large salad, Alex, Lukas, and Letti were greeted at the door by Magnus and Nancy. Alex took a deep breath. She wondered why she convinced Lukas to go to dinner. But she reminded herself Lukas wanted to be part of his father's life. She also understood Magnus didn't want to be alone. There had to be a way to fix things.

Nancy in all her colors, literally all the colors crammed into her dress, shoved her way to the front door.

Alex handed her the salad.

"You didn't need to bring anything." Nancy said. "I've made a wonderful spinach and strawberry salad with candied walnuts." She pointed at Alex's spinach salad. "I don't do mushrooms. I'm allergic."

Alex took the bowl from her and placed it on the step outside. "I didn't know."

Magnus rushed them in and hugged Alex. "Thank you for coming. I wish the other two had been able to come. Jens is traveling, and Nora had a soccer tournament with one of the kids, or two of them, I'm not sure. She's an amazing mother, managing everything she does."

Alex nodded. "Right? She's also grew her business and now has an online boutique. They opened a new warehouse to store all clothing. Rockstar. She takes after Bessa."

Nancy cut into the conversation. "We spent the entire weekend at our grandson's baseball tournament a few weeks ago. They placed second. It was so much fun, wasn't it Magnus?"

"That boy will get a full ride when he goes to college," Magnus said.

Alex watched Lukas tense up. Magnus missed all of Letti's activities. "What can I help you with, Nancy?" Alex rubbed Lukas on the shoulder as she passed him on her way to the kitchen.

"Oh nothing, I have a few snacks out for us while I wait for the steaks. I made our traditional Christmas meal since we've missed you over the years."

Letti sat next to the appetizers. "I've given up meat for a project at school."

Alex wrinkled her nose.

"Starts today," Letti raised her eyebrow.

"Granny wrapped the steak in bacon, your favorite," Nancy reached over the counter to pinch Letti's cheek.

Letti leaned back. "Should Grandpa be having all that red meat and bacon right after his heart attack?" She grabbed a carrot from the veggie tray and slid off her chair. "Cribbage, Grandpa?"

"Sure." Magnus reached into a cupboard full of games in the living room.

Nancy opened the stove. "Dinner will be ready soon. Magnus, love, will you get Crissy?" Crissy was Nancy's only daughter.

Lukas walked toward the door on the side of the house.

Nancy took the steaks out of the oven. "She moved in a few weeks ago. She's clean and we are working on getting her back into her kids' lives. They are with their dad. He's an ass. Magnus has been a rock. Helping me so much. I couldn't do it without him."

Lukas snuck out of the kitchen and outside to their covered deck.

Nancy nodded toward Lukas. "I'm sure he blames me for his father's heart attack."

Alex shrugged her shoulders. "I can't answer for him."

Crissy and Magnus emerged from the basement. Her hair was bleached out so badly that even cutting it wouldn't help her split ends. She wore a black tank with gold letters that read, Drama Queen.

She set her pack of cigarettes on the ledge next to the stairs. "Well, what do we have here? It's the perfect family with their perfect daughter." Crissy looked Alex up and down. "Where's your hubby?"

Lukas stuck his head in back in. "Hello, Crissy."

She huffed, "Where's the rest of the family?"

"Just us," Lukas said. "Your kids coming?"

"No."

"How are they doing?"

"See, Mom. This is the shit I'm talking about. He knows I lost custody, and he asks anyway. I'm fucking trying, I really am."

Lukas put his hands up. "Look, I'm trying to make small talk. I thought since there was the big baseball event everyone went to, you would have seen your kids, too."

"We're working on getting visitation for Crissy." Nancy said. "Crissy, honey, we are all so proud of you, aren't we, Magnus?"

"They don't need to know my fucking life story, Mom."

Magnus asked Alex, "Ready to eat?"

They gathered at the table and sat. Nancy stood behind her chair. "Let's hold hands and pray." Alex took Letti's hand with her right and Crissy's with her left. "Come, Lord Jesus, be our guest, and let these gifts to us be blessed. Thank you for gathering our families together, for Crissy's sobriety, and having our son back at our table. Amen."

Lukas and Letti made the sign of the cross. Nancy put the largest piece of meat onto Magnus' plate and took the smallest for herself before passing the platter to her daughter. "We miss getting those sausage samples, Alex. Are you still selling them?"

"Yes, I am," Alex answered.

"You must bring us some. Magnus loves that chorizo."

Crissy handed Alex the plate of meat and Alex asked Lukas, "Want to split one?"

Nancy answered for him. "Oh, no. This is make-up for all the Christmases missed. He should have his own."

Alex slid a piece of meat onto her plate, passed the meat to Letti, who handed it to her father without taking any.

"Letti, dear. Take some meat. I made this as a special dinner. I'm sure you can start your vegan thing later."

Lukas set the plate down and told Alex, "I'd love to split that with you, Alex."

Alex cut it in half and asked Letti, "Can you hand me Daddy's plate?"

Letti did as she was told.

The rolls, salad and green beans were passed around the table. Letti didn't take any of the green beans.

"Letti, you love Granny's beans. Why didn't you take any?"

Letti smiled. "There's bacon on them. I'm doing this for a school project. Can't eat meat for an entire month."

"Well, that's silly. What is this project about?"

"How people react to food choices. Are they supportive or do they criticize your decisions?"

"Oh." Nancy took a drink of her water.

"What else are you doing in school?" Nancy asked.

"I'm writing a paper on death," Letti said.

"That's odd. Should we be worried?" Nancy asked.

Magnus joined the conversation. "Actually, it's quite interesting. She has been asking people what they want done with their bodies when they die."

"Keith Richards snorted his dad's ashes," Crissy said, moving the food around on her plate.

"That's silly," Nancy said.

"Really." Crissy picked up the phone sitting next to her on the table. "Check out the interview." She hit play and so the entire table could hear Keith Richards talk about "ingesting his ancestor."

"Okay, okay. That's enough of that, we're eating," Nancy said. "Magnus and I will buy plots next to each other so you kids don't have to worry about us."

"We will?" Magnus asked.

"Yes, we don't want the kids trying to figure out what to do with us like they are with Julia. It's not fair."

Crissy took a bite of her roll. "I don't want to be cremated. I also don't want to be put in a box under the ground. I like the water. Maybe I can be taken to sea."

Letti leaned over and said enthusiastically, "You can. Your body can be wrapped in a shroud instead of being put into a casket. You need good weights to make sure your body doesn't float back up."

"What's a shroud," Crissy asked.

"Like a huge cloth," Letti said.

"That's what I want," Crissy said.

"Can we please change the subject?" Nancy asked.

Crissy took a green bean off her plate and pointed it at Lukas, "So where is your mom these days?"

He sighed, "In a purple urn."

"That's funny."

Lukas put his fork down and wiped his mouth. "I don't see how that's humorous."

Crissy stood, stumbled to the kitchen, grabbed her pack of cigarettes and toddled back. "You all think you're better than me, don't you? You, your perfect Pinterest sister, even Jens. He forgets he let me suck on his dick when our parents first started dating."

Lukas pushed himself away from the table, and his chair toppled over. "Alex, Letti, time to go."

Crissy lit her cigarette.

"Not in the house, Crissy," Nancy cried.

Crissy inhaled and slowly blew the smoke toward Lukas. "Might wanna grab your mom on the way out. I think she's stashed in the hall closet."

Nancy stood straight up. Her entire body trembled. "Magnus, *that* woman better not be in my house."

She stomped over to the closet and flung open the door. She pushed boxes aside and froze. Alex saw it too. The urn. Nancy screamed, a dark shrill. She took her hand and flung the vase off the shelf. It was like watching a scene in slow motion.

Alex felt stuck in place, she couldn't move. She couldn't stop any of it. Crissy took another drag, smirked, crossed her arms and spun around before leaving the room. Magnus reached out and said, "Jules. No."

Lukas yanked Letti away as the vase fell toward her. Bessa, The Urn, hit the floor and shattered. Glass, dust, and bone fragments scattered, crumbled, and flew back up into the air.

Nancy screamed again.

Alex snorted. She fell to the floor next to the broken vase. She let the ash run through her fingers, not worrying about the glass. Then she laughed hysterically.

"This is not funny," Nancy snarled.

Alex spoke through her tears. "Of course it's funny. You've tried so hard to be her replacement instead of just being with Magnus. You've always been so jealous. Julia's children had the best mom ever put on this earth. She loved them without hesitation, without limitations. She forgave everyone, even you. You will always be second, Nancy. And now. There will always be a little piece of Julia in your house." Alex placed her fingers into the ashes and rubbed them together. "There is no way you will ever find all the tiny granules. For us, we have a piece of her soul in our hearts forever. For you, ashes and bone fragments forever."

Nancy jerked the door open. "Get out of my house."

"I'm not leaving without my mom." Lukas towered over her. He backed up and stared Magnus down. "I'm not leaving without Mom."

Magnus was white. Not pale, white. He nodded and disappeared before returning with a broom, dustpan and a large glass container.

"Magnus, I put my sugar in that." Nancy argued.

Magnus scooped up the remains and carefully brushed them into the container. "Not anymore."

33. YOU SHOULD GO TO THE DOCTOR

Alex was the first one up. Like every morning the last few months, she had to take a trip to the bathroom and vomit. Usually she went to the basement so Lukas wouldn't hear her. But this morning she didn't make it. It terrified her that something was really wrong. She turned on the shower to drown out the noise, but Lukas tapped on the door. "You okay?"

"I'll be right out."

She looked in the mirror. Even she could even see she was pale. She splashed cold water over her face.

Lukas tapped on the door again. "Can I come in?"

Alex opened the door. "I either ate something bad or I have a bug. My stomach is a mess. I can feel the contents of last night's dinner swirling in my stomach."

"You should go to the doctor."

"I have an appointment."

"How long has this been going on?"

"Just started."

"When is just?" Lukas picked up the clock sitting on his

nightstand. "It's six thirty in the morning and they aren't open yet. When did you make the appointment?"

"Last week."

She pulled on a pair of pants, and they wouldn't button. She tore them off and grabbed a pair of sweatpants. "Having Fran around is not good for my waist. I'm getting fat."

"What time are they coming today?"

"Sometime this afternoon."

"Hopefully, the letter shows up today."

The letter didn't come like it was supposed to. For the past couple of weeks the four of them, Lukas, Jens, Nora, and Alex checked their mailboxes several times a day. Alex would check theirs even after she removed things from it, hoping the mail carrier would come back, realizing he'd misplaced it. Alex thought, *What if the letter had been lost? What if they would never know her last words?* She didn't say any of this to Lukas. But assumed he thought the same.

"Want me to drive you to the doctor?"

She shook her head. "I'll be fine."

"That's not what I asked."

"Why do you want to go with me?"

"What are your symptoms?"

"Nausea."

"Every day?"

"Yes."

"For how long?"

Alex turned the other way. "A couple of months."

"And your pants are not fitting?"

She put her hands on her hips. "Wow, are you calling me fat?"

Lukas smiled and asked a little too loud for Alex's liking. "When was your last period?"

"I don't know, why?"

"I think you're pregnant."

"I'm forty-four years old."

"Yeah, so?"

"We tried for years. It didn't work."

"So?"

"You're nuts."

"I'm coming with you."

ON THE WAY home from the doctor's office, they stopped at the grocery store. Alex had made a list for the weekend festivities.

Beans for soup
Chicken stock
Ham
Carrots
Onions
~~*Wine*~~
Decaf English Breakfast Tea (YUK)
Prenatal Vitamins

34. THE LAST LETTER. ALL OR NOTHING!

The letter had still not come. They gathered anyway. This year Magnus joined them and Margaret and Fran were on their way too. Alex made a big pot of ham and bean soup. The one Bessa used to make with lots of carrots. Nora brought cornbread, and Jens brought a bottle of vodka; a good one from Norway, named after a girl. They sat at the big table alone, without the food, without the kids, who were in the basement running around. The bottle of alcohol was in the middle of the table and they all stared at it.

The dogs barked, and tires on the gravel rolled up the driveway. Lukas stood, walked outside, and helped Margaret and Fran with their luggage.

Alex held the door open. "Come in." She observed Beth carrying a large box.

"We come with gifts. And letters." Margaret winked.

Lukas told Alex. "I told you she was part of this."

Alex's heart opened wide, allowing all the good to come in. "Maggie." She grinned. "He did. He knew you were part of it. I didn't believe him."

Margaret held a manila envelope and then waved it in the air. "Her lawyer sent everything to me. The letter asking me to do it, plaques for other kids as they were born for me to have engraved. It's it all in the car."

Beth sauntered in. "I have some of it right here."

Jens jumped from his seat and hurried over to her. "Let me help you with that."

She passed the box to him. "Mr. Chivalry now?"

"Play nice. I bought a great bottle of vodka."

"Got limes? Got tonic?"

"If you must."

She nodded. "I must."

"Be right back, I didn't bring either of those, but for you. I'll go get them."

"I'll come with you." She winked.

Alex tilted her head. *Something is going on with those two.*

Nora poked her brother in the side. "Hurry lover boy, I want to hear the letter."

Beth squeezed Jens' arm. "You all read the letter, I'll run out."

"I'll go with you," Fran said. "I'd like some wine to go with whatever is smelling so good."

Alex cringed. "Oh dang, that's what I forgot. Not sure wine goes with ham and bean soup."

"Wine goes with everything, Chica. What do you like? Syrah or..." Fran waited for Alex to answer.

"Surprise me." Alex wasn't ready to share her news. She was still in shock. Twenty minutes after they checked in, her doctor confirmed her pregnancy and an hour and a half after that, Lukas and Alex were looking at an ultrasound of what seemed to be a healthy baby, Alex was four and a half months pregnant.

Lukas chirped. "I wasn't ready to be an empty nester."

Alex stared at the monitor. “When the baby is twenty, I will be sixty-five.”

“So?”

The technician rolled the apparatus over Alex’s stomach. “Do you want to know the sex of the baby?”

“No.” Lukas covered his ears.

“Yes.” Alex squinted, trying to see if there was external plumbing. Why else would the technician ask so quickly?

Lukas took Alex’s hand. “I don’t want to know until the baby is born. I want to be surprised like we were with Letti.”

“This isn’t enough of a surprise?” Alex argued.

“Fine, we’ll let Letti break the tie.”

“Fine.”

Lukas let go of her hand. “Dang it. I just lost this one, didn’t I?” Letti normally took Alex’s side.

“Probably.”

“Alex?” Margaret said, snapping her fingers. “Where are you?”

Alex brought herself back to the present. “Sorry. Right here. How? When?”

Beth grabbed Fran’s hand and squeezed. “You stay. We’ll get limes and wine.”

Fran’s eyes widened. “Oh.” She winked at Jens. “Okay.”

Alex watched the exchange and whispered, “Something’s definitely happening.”

“Do you want to read the letter or not?” Margaret handed the letter she had received from Julia after her death to Alex.

Fran closed the screen door and took Alex’s arm. “Come on. You’re going to love this.”

Dear Margaret,

While it is not my place to interfere in your relationship with your daughter, dying gives people rights they didn’t

possess before. At least we assume it does. I think it does. I don't care about the 'ass between u and me' shit, either.

Remember the day the kids got married? You and I had wine. Too much wine. But what a fun day that was. We giggled and made fun of our ex-husbands and their significant others, and we talked about our children.

The love that you have for your daughter is amazing! Why do you bury it deep inside of you?

Are you afraid Alex will disapprove of your relationship with Francisca? I wish you had brought her that day. Alex shared with me she invited you both. Alex has spoken about you so much over the years. She accepts you for you. You raised her to be a good person and not to judge. It is my understanding your parents walked away from you when they found out you were in love with a woman. No parent should do that, I'm sorry they did. But you are doing the same thing to your daughter.

The thing is, I don't have time to candy coat this. So here are the facts as I know them.

1. *Alex loves you*
2. *Alex accepts who you are*
3. *Alex is happy you have found someone you love*
4. *Alex does not give a shit that the person you love is a woman*
5. *Alex misses you*
6. *Alex needs you in her life*
7. *Letti wants to meet her other grandmother (Letti and I have gone on Francisca's social media and looked at all your lovely pictures of you and her. She knows. OMG, and she doesn't give a shit either.)*

That's it, seven little things. Be in her life. Be the mother and

grandmother Alex and Letti deserve. They need you. I don't get to do what you can. Don't blow this!

Now that I've let my inner bitch out, I need to ask a favor. I have these letters I need to get to my children. I would have asked you while I was alive, but a dying wish is granted easier if you cannot tell the dying person no. I'm having my lawyer give you these. If you choose not to do this, just toss the letters.

I'm not a very religious person, but I've always held Mark 7:34 "Ephphatha!" (that is, "Be opened!") close to my heart. Now, people may not like my interpretation of this, but one day I was struggling with things. I opened my bible to the passage. I believe God was telling me to listen. To really listen. I did, and I had clarity. I hope you listen.

I would like the letters sent to my children, yearly...

You are the only one I trust to do this for me.

JENS AND BETH were gone for an hour. They walked in with produce for a salad, enough red wine for an enormous party, and pies from the local pastry shop. Jens used his fingers to comb through his hair. "We bought pies," he said.

Magnus piped in, "Did you get ice cream?"

Beth patted his tummy. "Not that you need it, I bought extra heavy cream and I will whip up some wonderful sweet cream."

Even though they were all excited to read the letter, they gathered, ate, and drank. All but Alex took extra portions, her wineglass was full, when she put it up to her nose to sniff the grapes, she thought she was going to vomit. She stood and went looking for the tonic water and poured some over ice and added a lime.

"Going for the heavy stuff today?" Jens asked as he grabbed a second helping of soup.

"Yeah."

Margaret pulled her aside. "Are you felling well?"

"I'm fine. I have Dad's stomach issues."

"Speaking of your father. Have you spoken with him?"

"Last week. He's coming out with his newest girlfriend. I can't wait to see how much older than Letti this one is. Gag." She stuck her finger in her throat.

"Gag? While I will never understand how you tolerate him, I don't understand the word gag."

Some things would never change, and Alex was finally okay with that. "He loves me, and he adores Letti. So we tolerate him."

It was Magnus who finally brought up the letter. "Can we read the letter?"

"Finally," Nora said.

Magnus stood, "Wait. Before we read it. I know what she wants."

"Who is she?" Nora asked.

"Your mom. I know what she wants done with her remains."

Letti grabbed a lime off the table. "You mean she doesn't enjoy hanging out in the sugar jar?"

Margaret shuddered and asked Alex. "Sugar jar?"

Letti answered for Alex. "When the urn broke, Grandpa swept her up and placed her in a sugar jar. Nancy's sugar jar." Letti giggled. "I doubt Bessa likes the sugar jar. It was Nancy's," she bit into the lime and chewed.

Margaret raised her eyebrows. "Don't chew on the lime. Citrus juice is bad on the enamel on your teeth."

Letti thought for a minute. "What about oranges?"

Nora moved closer to Magnus. "Enough with the lecture on citrus. What does Mama want?"

Magnus folded his hands together and leaned on the

table, “She wants me to save her. When I die, she wants our ashes to be put together,” he paused. Looked around the table. “Mixed. I don’t know any other way to say it. Then she wants us scattered on this property. If it’s okay with Alex, Lukas, and Letti. She doesn’t care if you sell the property one day. She wants to remain here, with me.”

The three kids nodded. Then Jens asked, “What if one of us says no?”

“Are you saying no? Any of you?”

They all shook their heads.

“She knew you wouldn’t say no.”

It was Letti that asked the other question, “Are you okay with that plan, Grandpa?”

“Yes. Yes, I am.”

On the front of the envelope, it read.

ALL OR NOTHING!

Hello, my most amazing children. Are you ALL here together? With your father? If not, get it together. You all have to be together to read the last letter. No exceptions.

Love you!

Margaret took the next letter from her purse. There was a heart on the front, inside the heart were their names written in different colors:

Julia in red

Magnus in black

Lukas in blue

Nora in pink

Jens in green

After showing them the envelope, Margaret said, “She asked me to read the last letter. Is that okay?”

After no objections, Margaret did just that.

My loves, my whole heart, you ALL are my entire heart. If my estimates are correct, it has been ten years since my death; I

hope you are happy. Wait! Shit. Letti is probably driving. Get off the road!

All joking aside, I want to thank Margaret for doing this. I sound like I'm at some award show. Weird.

In the end, things are simple. There is clarity.

Without you ALL, I am nothing. My world would not be complete without each and every one of you in it.

I love you. I will never be able to say that enough.

Love each other.

Stay with each other.

Never walk away from each other. You need each other. I promise.

Keep Christ close to your heart.

And by the way, I converted. Your dad would have wanted that. I made that priest keep it a secret, and I told him I didn't want a full mass. I didn't want you all to know then.

Magnus. I love you. I always have. I always will.

Yours for eternity,

Mom/Mama/Your beloved wife, Jules.

Margaret pulled out a box from her bag and handed it to Letti. Inside was a silver chain with the Miraculous Medal of Mary on it. Letti held it. A tear fell. "She used to let me wear this. I remember." Letti put the necklace on and then pressed it to her chest. "I love you, Bessa."

Margaret read the single card to Letti:

My sweet, beautiful Letti.

I don't think you will know how much I loved you. That breaks my heart.

Eli, six and sitting on Letti's lap, turned to her. His index finger touching his thumb. "I love you this much, Letti."

Letti stuck her bottom lip out and pretended to be sad. "Only that much?"

His fingers widened and with every expansion he said,

"This much, this much, this much," until his arms were wide open and everyone in the room yelled along with him, "Kaboom."

Letti squeezed Eli. "I taught him that. I don't remember who taught me."

Nora smiled. "Mama."

Jens shook his head. "Nope."

Magnus pointed to Jens and then back at himself. "You and me, kid. You and me."

Life is a gift. Treasure it. You have your entire life in front of you; you get to choose how you live that life. You can't blame anyone for your failures, well you can—but it doesn't work very well. Be kind, always. Be strong, always. Fight for what is right. Walk away from what doesn't matter or doesn't deserve your time. Thank God each and every day for your day.

Forever,

Your Bessa

P.S. Wear your seatbelt, Don't Drink and Drive, Don't Do Drugs. I have a list. There will never be enough time. Be good sweet girl, be good.

Letti looked up. "Thank you, God for my day."

THE FAMILY WORRIED that with Letti going to college, Lukas and Alex would start a new life, somewhere else, maybe downsize. Alex didn't want to be anywhere else. She looked at the family and then Lukas. "Are you telling them or am I?"

"Alex is pregnant."

Letti's eyes searched out Alex. Her eyes widened. "Yes!" She screamed. Then asked, "Really, you promise?"

"I'd shoot myself." Nora put up her hands. Then she bit her fingers. "Sorry that was really a shitty thing to say."

"It's okay," Alex said.

"How?"

"When two people love each other—"

"Really? I thought you couldn't."

"So did we. We were wrong."

Alex won, Letti couldn't wait to find out if she was having a sister or a brother.

Lukas extracted the envelope from his pocket; they had the ultrasound technician write it down. He gave it to Letti to open. She squealed, "I'm having a baby sister!"

Lukas stood proudly. "I love me a house full of girls."

Alex slid her arm into his. "He has to say that."

Lukas put his arms around his girls. "Nope. I don't. I wouldn't have it any other way."

35. AND I JUST MIGHT SAY YES

Alex rolled out of bed, she couldn't sleep.

Lukas shot up. "You okay?"

"We've only known for a short time that I'm having a baby. Calm down." The lights in the house remained off, but the sun peeked on the horizon, turning the sky all different colors. She remembered her father telling her a red sky held a warning, but she didn't believe in tales. Alex believed all the colors filling the sky meant only good things would come. The family had finally come together as one. All in the home that Magnus and Bessa built, even if only for a sleepover. They didn't love the house. Their love was for the home. It didn't matter who erected the four walls, the love and sometime the chaos felt within made this place safe.

Alex tiptoed into the kitchen. She needed water. Cold water. She stopped at the couch. Beth lay in Jens' arms. He was awake, watching Beth sleep. He smiled and whispered. "One day, I'm going to ask this one to marry me."

Beth nuzzled in. "And I just might say yes."

"I knew something was up with you two. About time."

Alex took her glass of water out to the front porch and watched the sun climb. The hummingbirds woke and their high-pitched squeak and the fluttering of their feathers zoomed past Alex's ear. The hummingbirds Bessa named Gwendolyn, whether male or female, found the nectar Alex and Letti put out a few weeks before. It was a tradition Bessa started and Alex made sure was carried on. Alex admired the sky. It was a perfect deep blue. "You did it. I don't know how you did it, but you did it. You made it all good. I still miss you." Alex put her hand on her stomach. "It makes me sad that baby Maggie will never know, see, or experience her Bessa. But she'll feel all the love from my mother. Thanks to you."

A hand touched Alex's shoulder. Margaret appeared with a cup of tea. "It's decaf, it won't taste as good, but it will have to do."

"Thanks Maggie. Can the baby call you Maggie?"

"No."

EPILOGUE

Dear Bessa,

I thought I forgot you. But today I found something. It brought you back.

So much has changed. Grandpa left the hag. I know what that is now. I don't know if I'd consider Nancy a hag. I believe she is an unhappy person who now understands what it's like to break up a family. Who does that anyway? Who dates a married man? Who stays with that man after he has left his wife? She is alone. I hear she has a new boyfriend, but that is boyfriend number three since Grandpa left her. She will never be happy.

If I ever get married, it will be to a man as loyal as Daddy, but as spontaneous as Uncle Jens. Who, by the way, got married to Beth. Beth is the funnest aunt. Don't tell Auntie Nora. They are trying to have a baby right away because they both say they are too old to wait. I don't think either of them will ever be old. They live in New Mexico and have the coolest house. Since they've been together, I go see them once a year.

Grandpa breaks up his time between us, Auntie Nora,

and Uncle Jens. He spends the most time with Auntie Nora. Daddy says it's because she tolerates him best. I think it's because she gave him his own room in their basement of their enormous house. He can hide down there.

When he's with us, he stays in the guest room upstairs. The first time he stayed with us for three months, I moved to your room in the basement. Daddy said I could. At first I thought he was being nice, but then I figured it out. If Grandpa was comfortable here, he would stay more. Daddy and Uncle Jens love him, but you will always be their favorite.

I'm glad I don't have to choose a favorite between my mom and dad. They are my rock, together forever. I would crumble if they separated.

Maggie, who is now three, has my old room. You would love her. She is full of energy and love. I thought I'd be jealous of her at first, but I love her more than anyone in this entire world. I'm going to London for my sophomore year of college. I'm excited to go, I'm excited to be close to Grandmother, but I don't want to leave my sister.

I was looking around my room today and I found the wooden block you gave me. You said it was you and me. I looked at the picture, an older girl and a young one. You and me. Me and Maggie. I closed my eyes, and I remembered the swing in the backyard. I remember being pushed. Pushed high. So high that my bum would come up off the swing. That's when my mom came into the room. I asked her if she remembered pushing me high on the swing. Me playing Mr. Blue Sky. Really loud. She did. But she said it wasn't with her, it was with you.

She said you would push me on the swing for hours and we would play music and I would sing. I asked her where the letter was. The letter with all the songs. Those songs, they were the songs we listened to on the swing in the backyard. But it was the block of wood that made me remember.

I saw your face today, Bessa. You said, "You and me." You pointed to the picture on the wood. Then you pointed to your heart and my heart. I know it was real. You're still here. And I'm not talking about that stupid urn that is probably sitting in the corner of my closet. Just kidding. Grandpa keeps it. He got a replacement for the one that broke, my mom tried to talk him into getting a metal one. He wouldn't do it. He takes you with him when he visits all his kids. This family is cray cray! I'm lucky I'm part of it. You are here in my heart. You're always with me, in the songs I sing. Every time I see a swing set, which I do often, and swing as high as I can.

I gave the block of wood to Maggie today. I told her, "You and me." I pointed to the picture on the wood. Then I pointed to my heart and her heart. But when I said the words, I didn't hear my voice, I heard yours.

I love you, Bessa.

Forever, Your Letti

ACKNOWLEDGMENTS

Always and first, God. Without Him, I am nothing.

Sirach 2:7-9

You who fear the Lord, wait for his mercy;
  and turn not aside, lest you fall.
You who fear the Lord, trust in him,
  and your reward will not fail;
you who fear the Lord, hope for good things,
  for everlasting joy and mercy.

Duane, you are my heart and my breath. I will forever be eternally grateful you chose us. Without you, we would not have the blessings of our family. What started with four has grown to twelve. And who cares if it wasn't in a traditional way! We are filled and blessed with love and chaos—just the way I like it. I'm ready for more. You are "my six", you always have my back. Thank you for always loving me and supporting me in every way possible. I love you.

My family. We all raise each other in some form or another.

It takes a tribe to write and publish a book. I'm so very

grateful to all who have crossed my path and helped me. Thank you to my critique group. Several years later, I'm finally publishing my story. Jodi, thank you for always being my cheerleader, you are a cherished friend. Thank you, Cate Byers, for editing my story. To the entire community at Rocky Mountain Fiction Writers and Pikes Peak Writers, there are way too many people to mention, but everyone who I have crossed paths with for either thirty seconds, or hours and hours sitting at the bar, you've inspired me.

Thank you, Daddy and Deb for telling me truths. I want you to know; I know the difference between your and you're —You're the best.

April and Jennifer, this all started with a funny conversation at work. I'm grateful for the camaraderie we shared. I miss spending my days with you two!

ABOUT THE AUTHOR

Photo by Cameron Radice Photography

Sheri Duff writes contemporary family drama with a splash of humor from her home in rural Colorado. Having grown up a city-girl in the suburbs of Denver, with her husband of twenty-plus years, she now finds constant laughs amid their new country lifestyle. Currently, Sheri waits impatiently for a new barn to hold her much dreamed of donkeys, which are sure to add to her stockpile of down-to-earth tales.

Made in the USA
Columbia, SC
27 April 2021

36617866R00141